Gordeous CONSORT

ok two of the beautiful entourage series

E. L. TODD

Fallen Publishing

Gorgeous Consort

Cover Design provided by Dinoman Designs
Copyright © 2015 by E. L. Todd
All Rights Reserved
ISBN-13: 978-1511910743
ISBN-10: 1511910747

Troy & Harper

Troy

Grocery shopping was a pain in the ass. I only had two arms to carry everything so I was limited to the essentials, mainly ingredients for my daily protein shake after a visit to the gym. I had a car, but parking in Manhattan was such a bitch that I'd rather just walk.

I walked down the aisle with a basket in my hand and searched through the shelves. I grabbed a box of Lucky Charms even though it had way too many carbs, got my protein supplement, a few fruits and veggies, and then reached the hygiene aisle. I grabbed the Head and Shoulders shampoo then stopped when I spotted the boxes of condoms hanging on the rack.

My eyes took them in and I just stood there. I didn't know what all the fuss was about, but they made me feel uneasy. Perhaps it was what they represented: sex. I hadn't had sex in over a year. I pretended I was a flirty playboy that met up with random girls and had a good time, and it seemed to fool everyone who knew me—or thought they knew me.

In reality, I just wasn't there yet.

But I didn't move. Instead, I stood there like a teenager buying their first condoms. The anxiety and guilt held them in place while they stared at the different choices. Lubricated, flavored, magnum...there was a lot of choices.

"Troy?" A beautiful female voice came into my ears and reminded me of a meadow full of wild flowers. Just the sound brought me back to a place I hadn't been in a really long time. I suddenly felt panicked, like I needed to escape. But like a cornered animal, I couldn't run.

I turned to Alexia, the woman I gave my heart to so long ago. She hurt me more than I could put into words. Even after all this time, I wasn't back to normal. Would I always suffer like this? But I had to keep a straight face and pretend she absolutely meant nothing to me, that she didn't ruin my life—literally. "What's up, sweetheart?" I asked with a cocky attitude. I grabbed four packs of condoms, over-the-top amount, and threw them into my basket. They covered the rest of my groceries, hiding my milk, bread, and protein mix.

She glanced down into my basket, clearly seeing what I just threw inside, but she didn't comment on it. Her brown hair looked like it'd been dyed, and now it had a slight red tint to it. It was soft, I could tell just by looking at it. I remembered the way it felt in my hand when I fisted it in bed. Her blue eyes jumped out at me, icy and blue, cold just like her stone heart. "How are you?" She wore a perfect smile, the kind that showed all her perfect teeth from having Invisiline braces as a child, and it irritated me that she was so happy. It pissed me off actually.

"I'm well. Just stocking up for the weekend." I indicated to the basket and the condoms inside. *Take that, cold-hearted witch.* "What about you, sweetheart?" There was condescension in my voice. She was nothing like a sweetheart, more like a bitchheart.

"Great," she said. "Just grabbing a few things."

Why did she come over to talk to me? It wasn't like we were friends. I never wanted to be friends. I'd only seen her one other time after we broke up, and she acted the exact same way, like we ended on good terms. Did she have the memory of a raccoon? She was never very bright. "I should get going." I just wanted to end this conversation. My heart was beating fast and my palms were sweaty. My grip on the handle to the basket was beginning to slip because of all the extra moisture. I hated the fact my body reacted this way. I hated the fact that I knew it would always react this way. I was in a vortex, doomed to live in the past forever. As ashamed as I was to admit it, I glanced down and looked at her ring finger. There wasn't a ring there, and that gave me relief. But that just made me loathe myself even more. *Why couldn't I just not care?* "I have places to be." I walked around her, keeping my cool and indifference.

"Wait."

I turned around, which pissed me off a million times more. Why couldn't I just walk away? Would I ever be able to walk away? "I haven't got all day," I said coldly. "Spit it out." A part of me wished she would tell me she missed me. Or that I looked good in the t-shirt I wore. But what I really wanted her to say, whether I would admit it to myself or not, was that she made a mistake when she left me. I lived for those words.

"Are you still an escort?"

Disappointment filled me, and then anger followed quickly afterwards. Of all things she stopped me for, that was it? What the fuck did it matter? "What do you think?"

"Is that a yes?"

I cocked an eyebrow, trying to be as rude as possible. "What does it matter, Alexia?" I hated saying her name. It didn't sit well on my tongue.

"Well, I have a friend who needs a boyfriend for her parents' wedding anniversary..."

Fucking. Bullshit.

"Go fuck yourself, Alexia." I turned and walked away. I clearly meant nothing to her. When she looked at me, she didn't see an ex-boyfriend. She didn't see the three years we spent together. I was just...there. When would I accept that she didn't care? When would I accept it without being hurt?

Ever?

***

After I stocked the kitchen with the groceries I just got, I lay on the couch and stared at the ceiling. The condoms sat on the coffee table, which would never be opened. I would just take them back but I didn't care about the money. And I would risk running into that heartless whore.

Now I had to find a new grocery store. That was a pain in the ass because this place was so close to my apartment. Now I would have to walk an extra half-mile to a different place. Then I would have to figure out where everything was all over again.

Ugh, I hated that bitch.

My phone rang so I pulled it out.

It was Danielle, probably calling me for a new gig. I silenced it then tossed the phone on the coffee table in the bed of unopened condoms. The last thing I wanted to do was work. It would be impossible to put on a smile and be charming right now. I'd just be a fucking asshole.

The screen lit up so I knew she was calling again.

Unable to find the strength to move a single muscle, I let it go to voicemail. Danielle didn't call me again so I lay still on the couch. Depression came and went so I was used to it. But right now, it was heavy. I was disappointed in myself for not being stronger. I was acting like a pussy, letting a woman break me like this. The simple solution would be to get over it.

But you think I haven't tried that already?

My thoughts lulled me to sleep. The sun was still out but it was quickly sinking outside my window. I still needed to go to the gym but I lacked a purpose at the moment. So I went to sleep instead.

***

My dreams were worse than reality. Incoherent visions came into my mind and I wasn't sure what I was experiencing. But like the sun finally peeking out from behind a mask of clouds, it hit me hard and right on the skin.

The Grand Canyon was the backdrop to my dream. Millions of years of evolution were imbedded into the dirt and rock of the canyon. Fossils were lined in places that couldn't be reached without ruining the integrity of the foundation, something so beautiful it seemed to be created by a god, not by erosion.

"Can you believe we're here?" Alexia approached the edge of the cliff, wearing shorts and a razorback top. Her long hair covered her shoulders and it moved in the light breeze. It was a warm summer day, but the morning dew still lingered in the blades of grass.

I smiled while I stared at her back, glad I could do something to make her voice carry excitement. My purpose in life was to make her smile, and every time I succeeded it made me feel high. "It's amazing, isn't it?" I came to her side and watched her face.

She ignored me. All that mattered was the canyon below our feet. Like gods looking over a kingdom, we stared at the world like it belonged to us. I grabbed her hand as I stood beside her. Her palm was warm, and the grooves from her fingerprint were obvious to me. That was how well I knew her, down to the intricate cells that comprised her body.

"I've always wanted to go here," she said. "Thank you for taking me."

"I'll take you anywhere you want to go." I stared at the side of her face, mesmerized by how gorgeous it was. The Grand Canyon was a work of art, but its beauty doesn't compare to hers.

She finally turned to me, and her eyes reflected the light of the sun. They were bright, like they were glowing just for me. Every time she gave me that look, I felt at peace. How did I get so lucky to find someone like her to share my life with? What did I do to deserve something as perfect as she? "Why are you staring at me like that?"

"Because I love you." There was no other explanation. It was the simplest way to explain the thoughts in my heart.

Her eyes were glued to mine, and she searched my soul. A strand of hair blew in front of her face, sticking to the moisture of her lip, and then flew away again.

The time had arrived, the moment I'd been waiting for. I pulled the box out of my pocket then kneeled.

"Oh my god..." She covered her mouth with both hands and released a loud gasp.

I snapped the box open and looked into her face, not feeling a train of doubt or hesitation. Spending my life with her was the right decision, and it would bring me nothing but joy. She was the one. "Will you marry me, Alexia?"

She lowered her hands and showed a wide smile. Her eyes watered with emotions, moved by the ring and the words. The Grand Canyon was a place she'd always wanted to go, and I couldn't think of a better place to declare my undying love for her. Seeing the joy in her eyes, the reflection of what I felt in my heart, made me realize just how lucky I was.

But then the scene changed. The sun disappeared as a blanket of dark clouds obscured the sky. It suddenly became cold and windy. The scent of rain came into my nose. Crows flew across the sky, releasing their annoying cries. The wind picked up and blew violently through her hair, obscuring most of her face. The strength almost blew me over and down the cliff.

Alexia stepped back from me, like my touch appalled her. A look of disgust overcame her face. The joy in her eyes that was there just seconds before was absent. She moved to a tall man with a face I couldn't distinguish. She touched him like she needed him, that she needed him more than me.

"Alexia?"

She clung to him and looked at me like she wished I would just go away.

The wind blew harder, becoming a wall of force. It pushed me further to the edge. I didn't fall over but my body moved. The box in my hands started to shake, like it wouldn't stick around for long.

"No." Her answer echoed on the wind, wrapping around me. There was no doubt or room for mistake. Her answer was clear. "No."

The wind pushed me harder and I fell over the cliff. But I grabbed the edge and held on. "Alexia?" I couldn't hold onto the ring at the same time so I set it at the end of the cliff. "Alexia!"

She slowly approached the edge and looked down at me. Now she stared at me like she despised me, like she wanted me to stop existing—forever. Her foot moved to the box and she kicked it gently, letting it roll over the cliff and fall off the edge.

I held on and watched it fall, hoping I wouldn't share the same fate.

She kneeled down and grabbed both of my hands.

She was pulling me up. I wasn't going to fall.

But a sinister glow came into her eyes. They turned red and maniacal. She suddenly looked like the devil, not the woman I loved. Demonic fire burned in her eyes, and it was clear she wouldn't be pulling me back up the ledge.

She loosened one hand on the ledge.

"Stop!" I tried to grab on again but she wouldn't let me.

"Why would I be with you?" she said in a deep voice. "When I could have him?"

"Stop!" I tried to grab the earth again.

She moved to the other hand, the last lifeline I had. "Why would I be with you?" she repeated.

"Alexia, stop!"

She gripped my hand with both of hers and gave me a final look. The anger disappeared and only resignation was left behind. There was no sadness, just obligation. She needed to throw me off and there was no other way. She had to get rid of me. "You are a fool." Then she yanked my hand loose and let me fall.

I screamed as I fell, looking up into her face as it moved further away. I kept falling, feeling the ground come close to me with every second. I was about to collide with the earth, to become a fossil just like everything else.

But I finally woke up.

"Fuck." I sat up, my body drenched in a cold sweat. I breathed hard and couldn't catch my breath. Invisible threads of the dream still moved passed my mind. I recalled all of it, including the way Alexia pushed me off the cliff. I wiped the sweat from my forehead and felt the shirt stick to my back.

Would this recurring dream continue indefinitely?

Was I doomed to suffer for the rest of my life?

Harper

I arrived at the restaurant first, so I decided to text my best friend Aspen, my personal cheerleader. *I'm so close to walking out of here.*

You can do it, girl.

My sister is going to be making out with her boyfriend every second, and then my mom will wonder why I don't have a man to make out with. I'm going to slap my mother. Like, actually slap her.

Harper, where's the girl who doesn't give a damn what anyone thinks?

I'm still here and I still don't care. But that doesn't mean it doesn't annoy the shit out of me. Aspen was supposed to talk me down, but if anything, I was only working myself up more.

You only see them a few times a month. Aspen's logical voice came through the words. *You can do it. And one day you'll find Mr. Right and they'll get off your case.*

Who knows when that will happen? My sarcasm was heavy and I was certain she picked up on it.

Just get through it. I'll buy you a drink afterwards.
Several. When have I ever only had a single drink?
As many as you want.

I put my phone in my purse then waited for the army to arrive. We were eating at an upscale place, and the pearls around my neck didn't feel right at all. I felt like a stuck-up prick. My family came from money, and the fact I didn't act snooty like the rest of them didn't bode well. I was practically a heathen to them.

My sister walked inside, tall with blonde hair, and her boyfriend Sebastian came behind her. They were holding hands. Apparently, they couldn't stop touching each other for even a second. I loved my sister and was happy that she was so madly in love, but damn, could they not be in love for, like, a second?

"Sissy!" she squealed when she approached the table.

I dropped my bitch face and put on a mask. "Kara!" I stood up and hugged her.

"You look so beautiful," she said with more energy than I could ever muster. Her positivity was annoying at times. I hated people who were happy all the time, nonstop. It just wasn't realistic. Or maybe I was just an extremely negative person. Whatever. "I love your dress. You look so thin."

It was hard to stay annoyed with her when she was always so nice to me. She gave me more warmth than anyone else in the family, and she always took my side when they ganged up on me. She was my friend as well as my sister, and the fact her life was perfect shouldn't be a reason for me to push her away. "You look beautiful too, like always."

"I couldn't agree more." Sebastian rubbed his nose against hers while looking into her eyes. Then he turned to me and hugged me. "But you're a close rival." His hug was full of warmth like my sister's then he patted me on the back before he pulled away. Affection was in his eyes, like he genuinely cared about me and not just because he was sleeping with my sister.

Kara put her arm around his waist and leaned into him, like she wished they were alone together. I suspected inappropriate display of affection was just on the horizon. Kara was tall, five foot eight, and she had beautiful blonde hair and a tiny waistline. She was a swimsuit model for a high-end company, and she was always known as the pretty sister. I didn't resent her for it since it wasn't her fault. I just wish everyone else would stop comparing us. Kara could do no wrong, and everything she did was successful. But my accomplishments were always overlooked like they didn't matter.

So annoying.

We sat down at the table, and I tried not to feel sad.

Sebastian had his arm over her chair and he was leaning close to her, sharing a whisper just for them to know. Love and adoration was heavy in his eyes. It was clear he was obsessed with my sister, cherished the ground she walked on, and loved her with his entire being. Kara obviously felt the same way.

Being in the presence of true love was painful because I was nowhere near having that. I would be lying if I said I didn't want a gorgeous man to look at me that way, that he couldn't keep his hands off me even a year after we'd been together. I tried not to be the bitter and self-absorbed person and just be happy for my sister, but sometimes that was just too damn hard.

"I love you," he mouthed to her.

Her cheeks blushed even though she heard him say that a hundred times. "I love you too," she whispered.

He cupped her face and kissed her, giving her a scorching kiss that was only appropriate behind a locked door.

"Okay...enough of that." They could be in love all they wanted but they could play tonsil hockey on their own time.

"Sorry." Kara released a faint chuckle. "Sometimes we get carried away."

Sebastian rubbed his nose against hers. "We need to learn self-control."

I tried not to roll my eyes in disgust. "What are you guys getting?"

That seemed to pull them out of their smooch-fest.

"The lemon chicken sounds good," she said as she looked at Sebastian's menu.

"Good choice, sweetheart," he said. "I think I'll get the same."

First, they had to share a menu, and then they had to order the same thing? *God, they're annoying. I don't even care if I'm a bitch for thinking it.*

Mom and Dad entered the restaurant. Dad wore slacks and a collared shirt, his usual attire even if he wasn't working, and mom looked like the first lady in her fine white dress that reached the area just above her knees. Her hair was in an elegant up do, and she held herself like she was the Queen of England.

Why couldn't I have a normal family that just went out for hot wings?

"Darling, you look wonderful." Mom hugged Kara and held her tightly.

Darling? My mom tried to act British sometimes and just couldn't pull it off.

"Sebastian, it's a pleasure to see you." Dad hugged him then patted him on the shoulder.

"You too, sir. We need to get together and hit the green soon," Sebastian replied.

"That's the best idea I've heard all day," Dad said.

Uh, hello? Do they not see me?

"How's the modeling going, dear?" Mom asked like a stuck-up prude.

"It's so much fun," Kara said. "They let me keep some of the shoes so I save so much money."

Mom chuckled and released a high-pitched, annoying laugh. "Every job has its pros."

Like she would know because she's never worked a day in her life.

"How's the hospital?" Dad asked Sebastian.

"Great," he said. "Juggling ten or more patients at once is difficult but I manage."

Sebastian was a doctor just like my dad. While Dad was a plastic surgeon, Sebastian was an emergency room physician. They had a lot in common, and of course, my parents loved Sebastian the second he told them what he did for a living. So my sister landed a handsome doctor for a boyfriend, and probably a husband very soon.

No one cared about what I did for a living.

Mom finally moved to me. "Hello, Harper." She hugged me but it was slightly less warm than the affection she gave Kara. I always felt like the lesser-loved sibling. I tried not to let it bother me, but sometimes it just got under my skin.

"Hey, Mom. I like your dress."

"Thank you." She didn't compliment me back.

Typical.

"Hey, honey." Dad hugged me then patted me on the back a little too hard.

It irritated me that neither one of them asked how my job was going. I may not be a supermodel or a doctor, but I thought my profession was pretty cool. Being an interior designer wasn't easy. It was extremely competitive and difficult to make a living at. *But no, no one in my family was impressed by that—except Kara.*

We sat down at the table and picked up our menus. Naturally, my parents asked Sebastian about every detail of his life, including his beach house in the Hamptons.

I liked Sebastian a lot because he was successful and good-looking, but the thing I cared most about was the fact he was so humble about it. He seemed oblivious to his qualities, but my sister was the exact same way so they fit together perfectly.

Then my parents asked Kara every detail of her life. Bubbly and buoyant like usual, she let them interrogate her without a hint of annoyance. Then the conversation went back and forth between Kara and Sebastian.

I didn't feel like being interrogated but I felt annoyed that I was left out.

"How's the business, Harper?" Kara said with interest. She was the only person who seemed to genuinely care.

"Good," I said. "The office looks nice and more clients are rolling in."

"You need to do my apartment next," she said. "I'm terrible when it comes to decorating. I couldn't even decide what color bed comforter to get. That's how pathetic I am."

"That doesn't mean you're pathetic, baby." Sebastian rubbed her shoulder. "I loved the curtains you put up in my living room."

He was probably lying but he hid it well. My sister was great, but she did have horrible sense when it came to decorating and matching. One time she wore a thick vest with shorts.

No wonder why she was a swimsuit model.

Sebastian turned to me. "Congratulations, Harper. Being an interior designer in Manhattan is quite an accomplishment. That's probably the most competitive field you can get into."

Thank you. I wanted to glare at both of my parents. "Thanks...I really enjoy it."

"So cool," Kara said. "Next time my model friends redesigns their apartment, I'll recommend you."

"Thanks," I said.

"Very nice," Mom said, but it was only half-asked.

Dad asked Sebastian another question about medicine, and I knew my time to shine was over.

I sipped my wine and tried to pretend I wasn't seething.

Mom turned to me, and judging the look in her eyes and the way her lips were pressed tightly together, she was going to interrogate me about my personal life—like usual. That seemed to be the only thing she cared about. If

I had a serious boyfriend, would she actually start to like me? Or only if he was a doctor or a lawyer?

"So, any men in your life?" she asked tersely, like she already knew the answer.

"No." I sipped my wine again.

Dad turned to me, like he was somewhat interested in the conversation.

"No dates or anything?" Mom asked.

"No," I said. "Too busy with work."

Judging the look on her face, that was the wrong thing to say. "Then you need to make time, Harper." When she said my name like that, I knew she was irritated. "Your younger sister seems to make time for it."

Don't hit her. Don't hit her.

"Mom," Kara interrupted. "Harper will find Mr. Right when it's meant to happen. Don't worry about it."

I could kiss her.

"Have you tried online dating?" Mom asked.

Getting dates wasn't hard. It was finding the right date that was impossible. "Mom, how's the charity foundation going?"

She rambled on about that for a while. Changing the subject only worked if you were somewhat complimenting the person's ego.

When I glanced at Kara, she winked at me.

At least I averted the crisis—for now.

***

After dinner was finished, I was excited to leave. I could only handle my parents in small doses. Kara and Sebastian were angels compared to them, but even they were annoying—unintentionally.

18

I kept eyeing the waiter, hoping he would bring the tab over so we could pay and get it over with. He kept moving around to the other tables, clearly too busy to slip us the bill.

Ugh.

Sebastian cleared his throat then adjusted his chair, sliding away from Kara. "There's something I want to say and...I think now is the time to say it."

What? What did I miss?

My parents were both silent, and my mom's eyes started to water.

Holy shit. Sebastian is going to propose.

Sebastian lowered himself to one knee and extended a tiny box. "Kara, you are my life and the other half of my soul. It's only been a year but I don't need more time. You are what I want forever. So please be mine."

You've got to be kidding me.

Kara's eyes immediately filled with tears. "Oh my god..." She waved the moisture away but it didn't help. "Oh my god..."

Sebastian smiled at her response but his eyes were just as full of emotion. He took the ring out of the box, and before waiting for her answer, he slid it onto her finger.

"It's so beautiful," she said through her tears. "I love it. I love you."

Goddammit, my eyes are starting to water. The hopeless romantic in me was coming out.

"I love you too." He cupped her face and kissed her, still on one knee.

Everyone in the restaurant started to clap and whistle.

Mom dabbed at her eyes with a napkin. "So beautiful..."

Even Dad was a little choked up.

Sebastian returned to his chair and held her close. "Thank you for doing me the honor of saying yes."

"Thank you for proposing," she said while she blubbered.

"We're so excited to have you in our family, Sebastian," Mom said emotionally.

"Now we finally have a son," Dad said.

Kara and Sebastian were in their own world, the love leaking out of every poor in their body. Watching them stare at each other with nothing but love in their eyes was a beautiful thing to watch. There was no doubt on either side, and there certainly wasn't any possibility they wouldn't last forever. I was so happy for my sister. She was one of the rare people in the world who was gorgeous on the outside, but also gorgeous on the inside. She deserved a man like Sebastian. I finally forgot about my own pain and just basked in her joy.

When they finally broke apart, Kara turned to me. "You'll be my maid of honor?"

Then the happiness drained from my body. Weddings were a joyous time, but it would also be the time where everyone would wonder why I, the older sister, didn't even have a boyfriend. They would pity me, the older, less attractive sister. And I would have to deal with this every day until the wedding was over. But I put that aside, knowing I couldn't be selfish. "I'd be honored."

***

As soon I got out of there, I headed to my favorite bar and took a seat in the stool. Then I tapped the wood to get the bartender's attention and ordered something strong. "Gin and coke. Make it a double."

"You got it, lady." The bartender slid the drink to me.

I downed half of it, felt the burn in my throat, then set the glass down. My stomach was immediately warm and some of the edge was off. When I thought about this wedding, I realized how much of a pain it was going to be. I was happy for my sister, but I would pretty much be a punching bag to everyone else.

"Drinking alone on a Thursday night?" a familiar male voice said. "Pretty pathetic."

I turned and watched Troy sit in the stool beside me. "I don't see you with anyone."

"Really?" He held up his beer. "I beg to differ."

"Then I'm not alone either." I held up my glass. "And my company is better than yours."

"It's stronger, I'll give you that." He rested his arms on the counter, and his large arms were noticeable even in the darkness. Troy had a lean body but it was ripped with muscle. I noticed it the first time I laid eyes on him. But my attraction didn't go past that.

"So, why are you here alone?" I asked casually.

"You go first."

I set my glass on the coaster. "How will I know if you'll answer after I do?"

"Because I'm not a dick."

I cocked an eyebrow.

"Okay, I'm not a *huge* dick."

"Just a small dick?" I teased.

A small grin broke out on his face. "You tell me. Is eight inches small to you?"

21

I drank my glass without looking at him. I wanted to hide the redness in my cheeks. Eight inches sounded perfect to me. I hadn't had a good lay in a while, and Troy seemed like a guy who could do a decent job.

"I doubt you could handle eight inches," he said. "You're so tiny."

"Just because I'm small doesn't mean I can't handle something big."

"Really?" A cocky attitude stemmed in his eyes. "Let's find out." He leaned toward me, the scent of his cologne lingering in the air. His bicep touched mine, and I noted the heat searing his skin.

I turned in my seat and faced him. "You know what I think?"

"That we should head to the bathroom?" That smirk was still on his face, and I hated the fact I liked it.

"I think you're all talk."

He released a sarcastic laugh. "Just lift up your shirt and I'll prove my size isn't all talk."

"That's not what I meant."

"Then what did you mean, sweetheart?"

I didn't like it when he called me that. The word wasn't offensive. It was just the way he used it. It was full of sarcasm and annoyance. It seemed like a term he used to subtly insult someone. "I'm not your sweetheart so don't call me that. My name is Harper."

"I like nicknames," he said. "Like Battleship."

Battleship was Aspen's nickname. And it stuck to her like glue. "Then pick a different one."

"Okay." He rubbed his chin as he thought for a moment. "I need to know more about you to pick the right one—preferably in the bathroom."

"Like I said, you're all talk." I challenged him with my eyes as I took another drink.

He suddenly turned serious. That smile I loved and hated disappeared off his face like a clean chalkboard. It was gone, but some of it subtly remained. His eyes lost their playfulness. "Yeah? Why is that?"

"I've seen you around a lot, Troy. You never leave a bar with a girl."

"I'm picky." He drank his beer and didn't look at me.

"You're so picky that you never pick up a girl?" I asked incredulously.

"Who said I never pick up girls?" he demanded. "I go through chicks like sticks of gum. They taste good for five minutes before they grow bland and dull. Then I grab a new flavor and hope for something different."

I didn't know Troy that well, but I couldn't believe that. He acted like a tough guy but I knew he was just a big sissy underneath. Arguing was the last thing I wanted to do so I let it go. "So, are you going to answer my question?"

"Which one?" he asked. "You have so many." Irritation was obvious in his voice.

"Why are you here?"

"I told you to go first."

"Why do I have to go first?" I asked.

"Because you might not tell me the truth if it's the other way around."

"I'm not a bitch," I argued.

He cocked an eyebrow.

"Okay, I'm not a *big* bitch."

He took a large drink before he set his glass down. "Alright, you ready?"

"Ready."

"What we share between us is a blood tie."

"A blood tie?" I asked.

"It doesn't leave the two of us. You can't tell Aspen and I can't tell Rhett. Do we have an understanding?"

I extended my hand to shake his. "Deal."

"It's a blood tie," he said. "We have to seal the deal with blood."

"Well, I'm not a freak so a handshake will have to do."

He smirked then took it. "Alright, listen up."

I sipped my gin and crossed my legs.

"There was this chick I was with over a year ago. We were together for a long time, about three years. Long story short, she left me. It was totally unexpected and I never knew what I did wrong. Then I saw her about a week later with some guy. Everything became clear. Anyway, I just ran into her at the grocery store. She spoke to me like we were friends." He rolled his eyes and sighed. "Then she had the nerve to ask me for a favor. It took all my strength not to slap that stupid grin off her face."

I nodded. "That would be hard for anyone."

"I'm so over her and couldn't care less about her." His voice carried his bitterness. "But I hate her."

"You can't not care about her if you hate her. Hatred is a form of emotion, whether it's positive or not."

He gave me a dark look. "Don't try to analyze me, alright? I'm just explaining why I'm here."

"I'm not analyzing you," I said simply. "I'm just trying to help you."

"Well, I don't need your help," he jabbed. "Now you go."

Mine seemed totally immature in comparison to his, but a deal was a deal. "My younger, more attractive, sister is getting married. I've always been the older and less successful sister living in her shadow. My family has been hounding me to get a boyfriend for a long time and now that torment will be worse. I'm happy for my sister, but I just wished this happened when I was seriously seeing someone."

He didn't put me down like I thought he would. Since his situation was worse than mine, I expected him to say I was acting like a brat and I needed to get over it. But he didn't. "I feel terrible for women sometimes." He drank his beer in silence.

"Why?" I didn't expect him to say that.

"For women, if you aren't seeing someone seriously by the time you're twenty-two, you're considered a freak. There's obviously something wrong with you. If you aren't married or at least engaged by the time you're twenty-five then there's something seriously wrong with you. It's an unfair standard that shouldn't even exist. Why can't a woman be single if she wants to be? Why do people automatically assume she's unhappy? I could be a forty-year-old single man and no one would question it. But if I were a woman...different story." He finished his beer then left it on the table.

His words caught me off guard. Troy acted like a jerk sometimes but there seemed to be so much more underneath. But ironically, it seemed like he was trying to hide it most of the time. "That's the first time a guy has ever understood my problem."

"Well, Rhett and the rest of the guys would understand it too. Perhaps you forgot what we do for a living." He played with the coaster in his hand. "I've seen family be brutally mean to some of the women I escort. The fact she doesn't have a boyfriend or husband doesn't make her a bad person. It doesn't change her at all, actually. Its just unfair." He shook his head at the end.

I rested my elbows on the table. "Thanks for being understanding."

"Yeah."

"Are your parents that way with you?"

"Not really," he said. "But like I mentioned, men and women have different expectations."

"Do you like being an escort?" I asked.

"I love it," he said bluntly. "Don't get me wrong, there are some things I hate, like women getting clingy or ex-boyfriends chasing me with a steak knife, but those are just working hazards. The rest of the time I really enjoy it. I've helped a lot of people find peace with their familial situations. The day they no longer need me is what I look forward to the most."

I assumed escorting was just a way to get money. I didn't realize Troy actually cared about what he did. Again, it was a soft side to him that I'd never seen before.

"It sounds like you might need our services," he said. "To get you through this wedding."

"Maybe," I said. "But my sister just got engaged so I doubt there will be any wedding planning for at least a few months. I'm safe for now."

"Why don't you just get a boyfriend?" he asked.

I turned to him with an incredulous look on my face. "And you think that's easy?"

"For you I'm sure it's a walk in the park."

What did that mean? "Excuse me?"

"Harper, you're a perfect ten. You could get any guy you want."

Perfect ten? "You check me out?"

"Did you think I was gay?" he countered. Then that grin returned to his face. "I've checked out your ass a few times. It's nice."

Something like this would normally offend me, but coming from Troy it didn't. And there wasn't an explanation. "Finding a date isn't hard. But finding someone to love and have a meaningful relationship with is different. Believe me, if I could have a love like my sister and her fiancé, I would. I wouldn't be drinking alone right now."

"Relationships aren't all they're cracked up to be." There was a deep sadness in his voice. He sounded completely different than usual. "If you think finding Mr. Right is going to fix all your problems, it won't. The only person who can truly make you happy is yourself."

"I don't have any problems that need to be fixed," I countered. "I just want to find someone to share my life with. If you say you don't want that too, you're lying."

He turned to me and there was a cold look on his face. "I don't." There was determination in his eyes, like he was challenging me to disagree or call him a liar. I didn't make that mistake.

"She really fucked you up, didn't she?"

He didn't react whatsoever. "No. She helped me see the light, actually."

"Not all girls are like that, Troy."

"Yeah?" There was doubt in his voice.

"You like Battleship, right?" I asked. "You think she's good for your friend Rhett?"

"I don't have a problem with her," he said vaguely.

"You really think she would hurt him the way this girl hurt you?" My question hung in the air for a long time. "Because she wouldn't. Don't let one bad relationship ruin all your potential relationships."

He turned to me, irritation evident in his blue eyes. "Don't tell me how to live my life or how I should feel. I could easily sit here and tell you to get over yourself and your insecurities. Maybe your sister is prettier than you, and maybe she is more liked by your family. But you need to let it go and stop caring what other people think. You need to realize your value isn't based on your partner, but whom you are inside. Do you want me to say that to you?"

I didn't answer the question, understanding it was rhetorical.

He threw cash on the counter then stepped away. "Have a good night, sweetheart."

"I told you not to call me that."

"It'll suffice until I find a better name for you."

Troy

It took me about a week to get back to normal. Every night, nightmares would come to me, and they were always the same. Alexia wouldn't leave my thoughts. She dumped me over a year ago but I couldn't get over it. I felt pathetic and weak. Why did she have me by the throat like this? I felt like a dog that had been dropped by the side of the road. My owner didn't want me, but yet I found my way home just to make it back to her.

I didn't like this side of me.

Eventually, I calmed down and my mind wasn't s fuzzy. I wouldn't think about her because I wouldn't allow myself to. Every time I did, all it did was cause me pain. I wondered if she was with the same guy. Did they break up? Was she with someone new? Or was she single?

Why did it fucking matter?

I wished I'd never walked into that grocery store. I wouldn't have gotten drunk and spilled my secret to Harper. Even Rhett didn't know the truth. He knew Alexia and I had a bad breakup but didn't know anything beyond that. But Harper seemed trustworthy. I couldn't imagine her breaking her promise and blabbing to Aspen.

I did find Harper immensely attractive. She wasn't like other girls. There was something different about her, but I couldn't quite put my finger on it. A confidence possessed her, and she took up the whole room even though she was five feet tall. She was blonde with blue eyes but she seemed unique to me. There was a distinct curve to her lips. Even when she was frowning, it was still there. I could watch the shape of her lips forever if it didn't make me seem like a weirdo. When I invited her to the bathroom, I really wanted to get down and dirty. But knowing me, we just would have made out and I would have chickened out, like always. The fact Harper called my bluff was actually a good thing. She was a close friend with Aspen, and it wasn't smart to get involved in something messy like that. Rhett was my best friend and I wouldn't undercut him like that.

But she did have a nice ass.

I was working that evening, so I put on my slacks and collared shirt and picked up my date. When I arrived at the door, I cleared my mind of my attraction to Harper and my pathetic weakness toward Alexia. Then I knocked.

Nate opened the door immediately. "Hey, right on time."

"When am I ever late?" I put on a fake smile and pretended to be the date he paid me for. My problems weren't his problems, and I left them at the coat rack.

He adjusted his tie before he stepped out and locked the door. "I'm nervous...like always."

"There's no reason to be nervous."

"My parents are never going to accept me." He seemed genuinely terrified. It was obvious in his eyes and his tense shoulders.

"Don't think like that," I said firmly. "It will get better."

"I have to keep trying," he said. "I don't have any other choice anyway."

I clapped his back. "That's the spirit."

He released a faint smile but it didn't seem genuine. "Thanks for helping me out. I appreciate it."

"No problem, man. It's what I'm here for."

***

We arrived at the restaurant where Nate's parents were waiting. They were talking quietly to one another, but judging the stressed looks on their faces, they were arguing about their son. Apparently, it was extremely inconvenient he was gay. He was their only child, and they were having a hard time accepting it. Nate hired me because he wanted to have a professional to break the ice. He didn't want to put a real boyfriend through the drama. It made sense to me.

We sat down in the chairs facing them, and it was immediately tense. They both looked at me like I was a nuisance, like I was the one responsible for all their problems. If I weren't in existence, their son wouldn't be gay. I'd never been so persecuted by strangers before. It made me have more empathy for Nate and the long road ahead. "Hello," I said politely. "It's nice to see you again."

"Yeah," his dad muttered.

His mom didn't say anything at all.

Nate looked mortified.

At least I was taking the burden off of him. That's what I was paid to do, to make his life easier.

An awkward stretch of silence passed. No one looked at their menus or made small talk about the weather or traffic. They just stared at me like they wish I were hit by a cab on the way here.

"How's it going?" Nate asked in an attempt to break the ice.

His parents finally turned their attention on him.

"I've been better," his mom said coldly.

His dad eyed his wife and son.

Nate rubbed the back of his neck, clearly unsure what else to do.

"I went to Nate's play the other night," I said. "He did an amazing job." His parents didn't approve of Nate being a dancer. It wasn't 'masculine' enough. But they were missing out on all the amazing things their son could do. It was a shame.

"You guys should come next week," Nate said hopefully. "I can get you good seats."

Like his mom hadn't heard a word he said, she spoke quickly and with a panicked voice, like she'd been holding her thoughts in for a long time. "We found this therapist here in Manhattan. We want you to see him on Monday."

I tried not to sigh at the blow. Just the fact they met me here tonight meant they were more open to Nate's personal life. But if they were advising this, that Nate needed professional help, then they weren't open at all. Every time we took a step forward, we took a zillion steps back.

"A therapist...?" Heartbreak was heavy in Nate's voice. He sounded devastated, beyond hurt, that his parents disapproved his life so much that they resorted to this idea.

It broke my heart too.

"Yes," his dad added with a strong voice. "You can talk to him about this and realize it's just a phase. Every one gets lost sometimes, son. We just need to find our way back. He can help you."

"I'm not lost," Nate said firmly.

His mom sighed. "Honey, you—"

"No," Nate argued. "I've been gay my whole life. Do you have any idea how much courage it took me to come out? And now you want me to go back in the closet? With the help of a professional? You want to hide who I am for the rest of my life because that would make you happy?" He shook his head like he couldn't handle his own words.

I turned to him with pride in my eyes. Then I patted his shoulder, silently telling him I was there and we would get through this. He returned the look with gratitude.

"Get your hand off my son." His dad's threat washed over me and left an oily residue on my skin. It rubbed me the wrong way, that some middle age man had the nerve to do anything but show me respect. He didn't want to go to war with me. Because he would lose.

My eyes turned his way, dark and brooding. I purposely left my hand on Nate's shoulder, being defiant. My affection was strictly friendly, but he was such a homophobe that he couldn't even understand that. I wasn't even gay but he only saw what he wanted to see.

"Did you hear me?" he snapped. His beady eyes looked twice as large through his glasses.

"Dad, come on," Nate said. "Back off."

"I said don't touch him," he hissed. "That's my son and I'm not going to let you mess with his head. You've already done enough damage. Now knock it off."

"Dad, I was already gay before I even met Troy," Nate argued. "Leave him alone."

"Your son is a wonderful man and human being," I said coldly. "It's a shame you can't see those qualities just because of what he does in the privacy of his bedroom. If you treat him that differently, then you obviously don't love him. The only person who should be issuing threats right now is me."

That set him off. He was out of the chair in a flash and coming at me around the table.

It would be my pleasure to beat the shit out of this man and disgrace him in front of the entire restaurant, including his wife. But out of respect to Nate, my friend, I couldn't do that. So, instead I was on the defense.

He threw a punch right at my jaw but I blocked it with ease. He growled then hit me again but I caught his fist and threw it down. I had the disadvantage because I was sitting down but I still took him like he was a boy at his first session of karate. His face turned red in frustration and he threw himself at me.

"Dad, stop!" Nate yelled.

"We're going to get thrown out," his mom hissed. She looked around the restaurant, clearly mortified by what was going on.

I quickly moved from the chair so he tripped and fell under the table. He didn't hit anything but the ground but I'm sure he felt stupid as hell.

Nate covered his face and sighed. "Oh god..."

"Honey?" His mom bent under the table and tried to help him up. "Are you okay?"

Nate threw his napkin down. "Let's go. This isn't going anywhere." He left the table and stormed outside.

I followed him and caught up to him when we were at the sidewalk.

Nate turned to me, his eyes distantly watery with shame written all over his face. "I'm so sorry…"

"Hey." I grabbed both of his shoulders and forced him to face me. "Don't apologize. You have nothing to apologize for."

"My dad has never been a confrontational person," he said. "I'm sorry he attacked you."

"He didn't land any blows so we're good." I gave him a smile. "Really, it's okay."

He looked down at the ground. "They're never going to let this go. And if it keeps happening…I might have to cut them out altogether. I hate my parents for the way they're treating me but I do love them. I don't want it to be this way." Emotion was heavy in his eyes and he was struggling to hide it.

"Listen to me," I said gently. "They're the ones choosing to miss out on things. They are the ones making this difficult. They are the ones refusing to accept you as you are. As much as it hurts to let go of someone you love, if they don't love you back, then you don't have a choice. If they never come around, it's their loss. You need to think about it in that way because you've already done everything you can to make this work. I know it hurts but…you have to let it go."

He nodded. "You're right."

I rubbed his shoulder. "I wish things could be different. I really do."

"Thanks for helping me," he said. "I just wish they were nicer to you."

"Hey." I gave him a firm look. "Don't worry about me. Worry about yourself. I can handle anything. It's what you're paying me for."

A slight smile formed on his lips. "I'm glad I decided to hire you. If I did this with a real boyfriend, he would have left a long time ago..."

"I doubt that," I said seriously.

"I know so many gay people who have parents that are immediately supportive. The day they confess the truth, it somehow brings them closer together. That's what I want. I want my mom to take me shopping and ask for my input on outfits. I want my dad to come to my shows and watch me dance. I just...this isn't what I want."

I gave him a look full of sympathy. "Sometimes life doesn't work out the way you want. But you can't let it bring you down. You have to move on and be happy."

He nodded. "Easier said than done."

"You'll manage," I said with an encouraging smile.

He hugged me for a moment before he pulled away. "How do you know so much about this? Have you had a lot of gay escorts?"

"A few," I said. "But my brother is gay. I've had to deal with a lot of bullshit from my family because of it. So...I know exactly how you feel. I understand all the frustration and pain. You aren't alone in your sorrow."

"Do they still not accept him?" he asked quietly.

I shook my head in response.

"I'm sorry."

"Thanks, man."

I put my arm around his shoulder, and together we headed up the street.

"You want to come to my show tomorrow night?"

Nate and I had become friends through this journey, and I didn't mind seeing him outside of work. He seemed perfectly normal, not obsessive like some of my clients. Plus, he was gay and he knew I was straight. So, I never had to worry about giving him the wrong impression. "I'd love to."

"Cool," he said with excitement. It clearly meant a lot to him that I was supportive. I could never replace his parents, but it was still better than nothing. "Can I have your number to text you the address and time?"

One of my rules was not to give out personal information. It just made things easier. But I didn't see the harm. I hung out with Nate because he was my friend, not just because he was paying me to spend time with him. "Sure."

***

Rhett and I sat together in a booth with our beers in front of us.

"How's it going with Battleship?" I asked before I took a long drink.

"Great." He didn't smile but his eyes gave him away. It was obvious it was more than great, and it was clear he was more than happy. Ever since he found her, he'd disappeared from the nightlife and parties. He'd rather spend the evenings at home with her. While I missed him, I was glad he found happiness. In the back of my mind, I knew it would end in heartbreak down the road, just like

37

my relationship with Alexia. But I didn't want to be a downer so I didn't remind him of that inevitable fate.

"That's all you're going to give me?" I asked incredulously. "Just great?"

"What do you want me to say?" he asked. "If I tell you how in love I am with her you'll call me a pussy."

"You *are* a pussy." I gave him a teasing grin.

"Thanks for proving my point."

"Come on, I really want to know."

He studied my face for sincerity before he spoke. "She's the one, man."

"The one?"

"Yep."

That summed up everything in a nutshell. "Are you going to propose soon...?" I really hoped not.

"No," he said. "I'm happy with the way things are. And it couldn't come at a worse time since she's taking over her father's company. She doesn't have time for that and a husband."

"And she doesn't care you're an escort?" I found that hard to believe. Perhaps I was just paranoid after Alexia, but I wouldn't want my girlfriend to be anywhere near another man.

"No. She trusts me. And she should."

Seeing how happy my friend was only reminded me how depressed I was. Alexia was my tormentor, and no matter how much time had passed, she wouldn't go away. Was I doomed forever? What did I do to deserve this?

"What about you?" He drank his beer and watched me.

I gave him the response I always gave him. "Nothing."

"You've been saying that for almost two years." There was a tone of disappointment in his voice.

I didn't want to talk about it, not even to him. If I just pretended everything was okay, then everything would be okay. Wouldn't it? Rhett was my closest friend but I couldn't tell him all my thoughts and emotions. That would be...too girly. "Well, there's nothing to tell."

He didn't seem convinced. "Harper is cute."

"She is." There was no doubt about it. That pretty blonde hair would feel good in my hand while I fisted it and kissed her hard on the mouth. She had the perfect height and perfect body. I'd always had a thing for short girls. It made sex a little awkward because I was so tall but that didn't make it any less enjoyable.

"That's all you're giving me?" he asked incredulously.

"What?" I demanded. "I'm agreeing with you."

"I thought something might be going on between you." He searched my face for a reaction.

"No," I said immediately. "I figured it would piss you off if I slept with her."

"How'd you figure?"

"She's Aspen's best friend...who's your girlfriend..." *Did he really not see where I was going with this?*

"I'm not talking about sleeping with her and never calling her again," he said. "Why don't you just ask her out?"

"Like, on a date?"

"No, deep sea fishing," he said sarcastically.

Dating was the last thing I'd ever do. Relationships were stupid and I wouldn't put myself in that situation again. I wished I could start sleeping around again, and eventually that day would come. But for now, I wasn't there yet. So, there was nothing I could have with Harper at all. "She's not my type."

He put his beer down on the coaster and sighed. "Okay, this has gone on long enough."

"Huh?"

"We need to talk about what happened with Alexia. I've been waiting for you to bring it up on your own, but the wait is over."

My heart kicked into overdrive and my palms were immediately sweaty. Did I not fool Rhett into thinking I was happy and moved on? Did he see right through everything? Did I have a false sense of security this entire time? "There's nothing to talk about." I spoke so quickly I was borderline incoherent.

Rhett didn't back off. "Dude, what happened?"

"Nothing," I said defensively. "We broke up. End of story. The end."

He cocked an eyebrow. "You're really pissing me off right now. Just talk to me. I'm not going to judge you if that's what you're thinking."

"You're really pissing *me* off right now."

"Did she cheat on you?"

He hit the nail right on the head but I wouldn't admit it. "I don't talk about my personal life because there's nothing to talk about." I slid out of the booth to leave.

"Then why are you running away?"

"I have a slut to fuck." I threw my cash on the table.

"I know for a fact you haven't slept with anyone in over a year. You think you're fooling everyone but you aren't."

I froze on the spot and suddenly felt weak. Did my plan completely backfire? Was I going around spreading lies when in actuality everyone knew I was talking out of my ass?

"Every time we're at a party together, you throw me at some girl and pretend you're hooking up with some chick, but when I find you, you're always doing something else. Why are you hiding from me? Just talk to me. How long have we known each other?"

I felt defensive that he knew my secret. But I would never admit he figured anything out. "You're totally off your rocker, man."

"Yeah?" Disbelief was in his voice.

"I can't even count the number of chicks I've been with. But that's none of your business. Why don't you just get off my case? Maybe you're happy in a relationship, but that doesn't mean I need to be in a relationship too. Not everyone is the same." I knew I was being unfair to my friend but I was too upset. It was easier to forgive someone for being wrong than for being right. I walked off without another word.

"Troy." Rhett calmly tried to get me to come back.

I kept going and walked out into the cold night air.

***

At lunchtime, I went to a nearby diner that had the greasiest and most delicious hamburgers in the world. Today was a cheat day, and I knew exactly what I would eat on my cheat day.

I walked inside and headed to the counter where I picked up my order. After I paid for everything I waited for them to return with the food. The curly fries alone were enough to make me come all the way down here.

While I was waiting, I scanned the diner and my eyes fell on a cute blonde sitting alone in a booth. With one hand, she held the huge burger and took a massive bite. Her eyes were downcast on a magazine and she wasn't even paying attention to what she was doing. A pickle fell out of the burger and fell on the plate. She didn't even notice.

Then I recognized her face.

It was Harper.

She wore dark denim shorts and a white top. Her skin was slightly tan from being outside, and her hair was pulled up in a casual up do. Her bright eyes looked dull as she concentrated on the words she was reading.

Since I was waiting for my order, I decided to pay her a visit. "Hey, sweetheart."

In mid-bite, she looked up at me. Slight surprise was in her eyes. After she recognized me, she took a big bite and chewed for a long time.

"You look like one of those hot chicks on those Carl's Jr. commercials."

She finished chewing then swallowed. "Like those models have ever had a burger in their life."

"Maybe you can be the first." I wiggled my eyebrows at her.

"Thank you for the compliment but I prefer to be a little chunky and be happy instead of starving myself."

"A little chunky?" I asked incredulously. "You're a perfect ten, sweetheart."

"Stop calling me that."

"I haven't found a nickname yet."

"Well, you better pick one out soon. I'm about to knee you in the balls."

"You wouldn't dare." I crossed my arms over my chest. "You would be doing a disservice to all the women in Manhattan."

She rolled her eyes. "Like any women have seen your balls..."

I bypassed her comment. "You want to be the first?"

She gave me an annoyed look that clearly said, "Go to hell."

I chuckled. "What are you doing?"

"Eating," she snapped. "What does it look like I'm doing?"

"Alone?" I asked. "Don't have many friends, huh?" A teasing tone was in my voice.

"I'm on my lunch break," she said. "And I'm too hungry to wait until I get my food to the office."

"What do you do anyway?" I asked. It never came up so I didn't have a clue.

"Interior decorator."

"I didn't know that," I blurted.

"That's probably why you asked..." Sarcasm was in her voice.

"That's pretty cool," I said sincerely.

"Yeah?" Distrust was in her eyes, like I was about to make a joke.

"Yeah," I said.

The worker came over with my bag of food. "Here you are, man."

"Thanks." I grabbed it and set it down. "Since you don't have any friends, can I join you? I feel bad making you eat here all by yourself."

"How sweet of you," she said sarcastically.

I moved into the seat across the table and devoured my food. "This place has the best burger ever."

"A cheap diner?" she asked incredulously. "You really need to try the upscale restaurants here."

"Too snooty for me." I grabbed my burger with both hands as I shoved it into my mouth.

She watched me eat, a disgusted look on her face. "Did your parents not teach you any table manners?"

"At least they taught me not to stare."

She rolled her eyes then returned her gaze to her magazine. Then she picked at the fries on her plate.

We sat in comfortable silence. I ate while I watched her across the table. I noted the curve of her lips, the quality that always got my attention. Her upper lip reminded me of the curve of a bow. They looked so soft and full. I had the distinct feeling she was a good kisser. Too bad I would never know.

"Look who has a staring problem now." She kept flipping through her magazine without directly looking at me.

"What else am I supposed to look at?"

She tossed a magazine at me. *Home and Whole.*

I cocked an eyebrow. "If it's not *Playboy* or *Maxim,* I'm not reading it." I didn't subscribe or read either one of those magazines, but she didn't need to know that.

"Maybe you should branch out a little bit. Just some friendly advice…"

I grabbed her magazine out of her hand then put it down. "How about you talk to your guest instead of ignoring him?"

"You're the one who sat down uninvited."

"No, I asked if I could join you."

"And what did I say?" she challenged.

Actually, she didn't say anything. But I wouldn't admit I knew that. "How long have you been a designer?"

"A few years," she said. "My business didn't take off until the past year, however."

"You have your own office and everything?" I asked in amazement.

"Yeah." She looked at me like I was the first person to show any interest in her profession. She was practically on guard, waiting for me to take a jab. "You really think that's cool?"

"Why wouldn't I?" I asked seriously. "Opening up any kind of business is hard in Manhattan. The fact you did it is totally badass."

Emotion overcame her face and she didn't try to hide it. She seemed to be in shock, floored by the words coming out of my mouth. She suddenly stiffened then looked down at her hands, like she was remembering something.

What did I say...?

It reminded me of Nate and every other person I helped. She just wanted to be loved and accepted like everyone else. "Well, I think it's really cool. You shouldn't care what they think because they're obviously idiots. You're badass, Harper. And really hot."

She gave me a genuine smile that reached her eyes. She was suddenly in a much better mood, like life had steamed inside her body and healed her. Like a wilted flower brought back to life with water and sun, she held herself high and proud. "Well, thanks."

"No prob." I kept eating, noting the sudden change in atmosphere. We were slightly hostile to one another before but now there was a comfortable connection between us. I studied her face while I ate, and even though she knew I was watching her, she didn't make a comment.

"Want to see my portfolio?" she asked.

"You carry it with you?"

"It's online," she explained.

"Oh, yeah sure."

She pulled out her phone then pulled up the website. "Scroll left. It shows all the apartments and houses I've done."

I sipped my soda while I browsed. I wasn't visually creative, and I always wore t-shirts and jeans because that was the only level of style I had. But I was immensely impressed by her work. Each residence had a unique style like it was carefully crafted for the owner's needs. "You have are a real talent, Harper." I handed the phone back.

She smiled. "Thank you. And thank you for not calling me sweetheart."

"It's temporary," I teased. "Don't get used to it."

She put her phone back in her purse. "It's astounding what people will spend on an interior decorator. It's so much fun and it's something I would do for free. The fact people are willing to pay someone to go out and spend their money is beyond me."

"At least it worked out in your favor," I noted. "Do what you love and never work a day in your life."

"Wise words, grasshopper," she said in an Asian accent.

I smiled because she sounded so cute in the attempt. "I just bought a beach house in Connecticut. You want to decorate it?" I was the laziest person in the world when it came to decorating a house. Only the bare minimum was there now; the couches, TV, and bed.

Her jaw dropped and her eyes were wide. "Are you fucking serious?"

I tried not to laugh at the shocked expression on her face. "Yeah."

"Like, oh my god, I would love to."

Her excitement was infectious. For some reason, her happiness gave me happiness. "But I've got to be honest. I have no idea what I want so I'll be difficult to work with."

"I've had worse so don't worry about it," she said quickly. "This is so exciting! When do you want to start?"

I shrugged. "Whenever you want. You probably should see the house first, right?"

"I would love to!" She was a whole new person when it came to her passion. She was bright and bubbly, not sarcastic and moody. I liked both sides of her, but I particularly liked this side.

"Cool. You want to go tomorrow?"

"Yeah, that'll be fun," she said. "But I don't have a car. I'm assuming you do?"

"Yep. It's an essential for my job—showing up in a fancy car."

"Awesome," she said. "When do you want to pick me up?"

"I'm off tomorrow so it's up to you."

"How about noon?" she said. "I do most of my work in the morning."

"That's fine with me," I said. "I sleep until eleven anyway."

She didn't make a jab at my laziness like I assumed she would. She took out a piece of paper and a pen. "What are the dimensions for your house?"

"You think I know that off the top of my head?"

"You know the square feet, right?"

"Seventeen hundred."

She wrote it down. "That's a good size. Why did you buy it, if you don't mind me asking?"

"Retirement. I'm going to rent it out as a vacation home. The days it's not rented out, I can use it. It's a win-win."

"Smart idea," she said with a nod.

"Thank you. I'm not as stupid as I look."

"I never thought you were stupid," she blurted. "A little annoying and cocky, sure. But never stupid." She gave me a teasing smile then packed her things in her purse.

I liked seeing her smile. "I think you're the first."

"And I think I won't be the last."

***

I pulled up to the curb in front of her building and she got inside.

"You drive a Maserati?" Awe was in her voice. She felt the dashboard with her palm then stared at the shiny gizmos in the center console.

"Girls spend all their money on make up and clothes. Guys spend it on cars."

"This is a sweet ride," she said. "Very nice."

"Thank you." Her compliment made me feel warm. "I have to have a nice car so I can show up to parties and events in style. But it's nice to have a regular person show some interest."

"Regular person?" she asked in offense. "I'm anything but regular."

I left the curb and joined the traffic. "True. My mistake."

She pulled out a notebook and pen. "Tell me the kind of things you like."

"Blondes, big boobies, tight pussies—"

"You know what I mean, Troy."

I gave her that cocky smile that annoyed her. "Be more specific next time."

"Tell me the kind of things you like for your home."

"I could give the same answer..."

She swatted my arm playfully, making me laugh. "I'm being serious."

"Okay, fine." I finally stopped chuckling. "I like dark colors, like black and gray. I have a more sophisticated taste. I'm not a fan of the modern look, you know, with red couches and a purple rug."

She made the notes. "Duly noted. Anything else?"

"I care more about comfort than looks."

"Good. That's important."

"And I want the room to feel comfortable. You know when you walk into a room and you just feel at home?"

"I do."

"Well, that's what I want. More people will want to rent the vacation home if they love the way it makes them feel."

"Excellent marketing skills." She made a few more notes. "I guess I'll have a better feel when we get there."

"You packed a bikini, right?" I asked.

"This is work, not pleasure."

"Come on, I want to see that perfect ten body in a skimpy fabric that barely covers anything." I nudged her playfully in the side.

She rolled her eyes but she was smiling at the same time. "No, I didn't pack anything."

"That's cool," I said. "I'm good with skinny dipping."

"We aren't skinny dipping," she argued.

"Be a little adventurous for once in your life."

"How do you know I'm not adventurous?" she countered.

"I can just tell."

She released a sarcastic laugh. "You obviously don't know me very well."

"Then skinny dip with me."

"In the ocean?" she asked incredulously. "People will be around."

"I have a pool."

She shook her head. "No."

"I'll change your mind..."

***

We pulled into the driveway then headed to the front door.

Harper examined everything with a designer eye. She was particularly impressed with the white fence porch. "This is really nice."

"Thanks."

"If we got some patio furniture out here it would look great."

"Well, since the beach is on the other side I don't think anyone is ever going to sit here..."

"But it's better than having nothing." She walked around the patio and looked around. "And have some flowers to lighten up."

"Which will die because I'll never water them..."

"You're awfully pessimistic, you know?" She crossed her arms over her chest and gave me a look full of attitude.

"I'm just being honest. I think dead flowers will look worse than no flowers."

"Who mows the lawn?" she asked.

"My landscape guy."

"Have them water the plants too," she said. "Problem solved."

"Whatever you say, interior designer." I unlocked the door and walked inside.

She walked across the hardwood floor and examined every crack. "Has this place been remodeled?"

"Right before I bought it."

"The floors are really nice—practically brand new."

"I got lucky," I agreed.

She walked around then rested her fingers on her lips. She moved through the house, checking every bedroom and bathroom. Then she returned and looked at the granite countertops in the kitchen.

"So...?" I sat on the couch and put my feet up.

"Okay, this is what I'm thinking..." She was in her designer mode. "Gray walls with white trimming. A white rug with black leather recliners, and colorful art on the walls to lighten up the place. How about that for starters?"

I shrugged. "Sounds fine to me."

"You weren't kidding about not knowing what you want."

"Nope."

"At least you're laid-back."

"I trust you, Perfect Ten."

She stopped in her tracks then her head snapped in my direction. "What did you just call me?"

I gave her a smirk. "I finally found a nickname for you."

"That's not a nickname," she said. "That's you objectifying me."

"Hey, it fits," I said with a shrug.

"Battleship is a real nickname. Perfect Ten is not."

"But it suits you so well." Before she could argue with me I walked outside to the back patio. The breeze moved through my hair, and the bright view of the beach was blinding to my eyes.

She followed behind me, and her argument dropped once she saw the white sand and blue waves. "Wow...this is beautiful."

"I know." I sat down in the chair and stared across the water.

When she looked away from the water she examined the patio and furniture. "This place looks perfect. I don't need to do anything."

"At least I got something right." I stood up and headed to the pool. I stuck a few fingers into the water. "Perfect temperature." I turned to her and gave her a smug look.

"Forget it."

"Come on, loosen up."

"I am loose," she argued. "Just ask Aspen."

"No, you're totally uptight. You're stressed about your family and your sister's engagement, you're depressed you haven't found Prince Charming, and you're pissed off no one gives you the credit you deserve. Do something crazy and let go."

"And I'll accomplish that by letting you see me naked?" Doubt was in her voice.

"Hey, this is a two-way street," I said. "You'll see me naked too. And don't act like that's not a treat."

"You and I have different definitions of treats," she said. "Getting a cranberry scone with my morning coffee from Starbucks is considered a treat."

"Well, I'm about to change your definition." I pulled off my shirt and tossed it on the chair.

Her eyes immediately went to my chest and she stared at my definition and hardness. The look on her face told me she liked what she saw, but she quickly looked away like she didn't. "You're wasting your time."

"You're going to make me skinny dip by myself?"

"I'm not making you do anything."

I undid my jeans and shoes and slid them off. I stood in my boxers, my thick thighs available for her to see. My hips made a noticeable V that disappeared into my boxers. There was no way she didn't like what she saw. "Come on."

She crossed her arms over her chest. "Why do you want to see me naked so bad?"

"I call you Perfect Ten for a reason." I stepped into the water. "I won't even look. Just get in."

"You're such a liar," she said with a laugh.

"Okay, I will. But get in anyway."

"This is a really odd friendship."

"It's our thing." I winked then stepped further into the water. "The water feels great..." When my shoulders submerged, I took off my boxers and tossed them on the concrete. "Are you as outgoing as you claim?"

She shifted her weight and looked at the sky. "I can't believe I'm even considering this..."

I splashed her with water. "Don't be a pussy."

"I have a pussy so why would that be offensive?"

"Just get in. Or I'll drag you in."

She shifted her weight again while she debated her decision. Then she released a loud sigh. "Fine."

"Yes!"

"But turn around."

"What?" I asked. "That's not fair."

"You took off your boxers in the water but I don't want to get my undergarments wet. They are really delicate."

That made my dick come to life. "Whatever." I turned around and didn't look. I faintly heard the sound of clothes hitting the concrete. I really wanted to turn around and take a peek but I held myself back. Then I heard her enter the water.

"See?" she said. "I'm crazy and out of control."

I turned around and swam toward her. "You're finally getting out of your comfort zone."

"Don't you dare look." She kept her shoulders below the water.

"I'm not." I came closer to her, hoping I could sneak a peek.

"I can see you, Troy."

"What?" My eyes moved back to her face.

She kicked me playfully under the water. "I have the same body parts all girls have. There's nothing special down there."

"I beg to differ. And don't act like you aren't trying to see my junk."

"I'm really not," she said seriously.

"You want to see my eight inches. I know you do."

"The pool is pretty cold," she said. "I doubt you're at your best right now..."

"There's a naked girl in here with me, whom I refer to as a Perfect Ten. The coldness has no hold over me."

She swam around and reached the deep end of the pool, where she could stand and keep her body submerged.

I really wanted to look, but she was staring right at me so I couldn't.

"Do you like my ideas for your house?" she asked.

"I do. I'm sure this place will look great."

"Then we'll get a photographer to take some good shots. When you put it up on a website, people will come flocking. And you can charge more money."

"I like money," I blurted.

"You don't say?" she teased.

My chest and shoulders were above the water, and the wind licked my wet skin gently.

"How's work?" she asked, changing the subject.

"Good." My voice didn't sound so enthused.

"What happened?" she asked bluntly.

I sighed. "It's a long story..."

"Well, we have all day. We're just sitting in a pool naked."

I chuckled. "My client is trying to get his parents to accept him as being gay. They aren't coming around and even suggested he see a therapist." I shook my head. "He doesn't deserve to be treated like that. I feel terrible for him."

"Whoa, hold on…"

"What?"

"You escort men?" she asked incredulously.

"Yeah," I said defensively. "So?" Did she have a problem with that? If she was one of those annoying homophobic people then I wanted nothing to do with her.

"I just assumed you only escorted women."

"Well, that would be discrimination." I was still on my guard.

"Troy, I don't have a problem with that. I think it's really sweet that you're so supportive of your client."

I relaxed. "Really?"

"Yeah. You're fighting for him and what he believes in. I think it's great."

Now all the anger disappeared. "His dad came at me because I touched his shoulder. I blocked his hits without charging him back. It was hard not to kick his ass."

"I feel so bad for your client."

"Yeah…it's unfortunate. At least he's getting through it with me. If I were a real boyfriend, it would be really difficult to handle. They're so disrespectful and make me feel like a criminal."

"You don't think they'll come around ever?"

I shook my head. "I'd be shocked if they did."

"That's too bad," she said. "He might need to cut them out of his life forever. But hopefully that'll make them realize what they're missing and get their heads on straight."

"Yeah, hopefully," she agreed. "That's really cool you guys are so cool about that."

I shrugged. "I guess I'm passionate about it."

She moved her arms through the water but remained submerged. She regarded me closely but tried to be discreet about it at the same time. "May I ask why?"

I noticed I told Harper more things than I told anyone else, including Rhett. Rhett tried to have a civil conversation with me about Alexia and the breakup but I just couldn't open up to him. But for some reason, whatever reason, I wasn't so closed off with Harper. "My older brother is gay."

She didn't react in any noticeable way. She didn't even seem surprised. "Your parents aren't supportive?"

I shook my head. "No. He's been struggling with it for a long time. It's really stupid that my parents won't just accept who he is. It's something that haunts him every day. I told him he shouldn't give a damn what they think, but naturally, he wants their approval. My parents just think it's a phase..."

"How long has he been out?"

"For years," I said quickly. "Which is why I don't understand why they won't just accept it."

"At least he has you."

"I'll stand by his side no matter what," I said. "He's always been there for me." And he was most of all when Alexia broke my heart and shattered my spirit. The heartache was painful and numbing, but the lost of a spirit was worse. I didn't know who I was anymore and I was far from finding out.

"My sister and I are the same way," she said. "She's a real sweetheart."

"Is she hot?" A grin stretched my face. I wasn't sure why I had to ruin intimate moments like this. I guess it was because I couldn't handle them anymore. They made me uncomfortable.

"If you think I'm a perfect ten you should see her. She's a model."

I couldn't picture her sister being more attractive. Harper was already perfect as she was. "A model, huh?"

"Yep. Swimsuit model."

"Whoa...for who?"

"*Sports Illustrated.*"

"Holy shit." There were tons of models in the city but I never kinda knew one.

"Yep. She has a short career but she's rocking it so far, putting away her money for retirement, not that she needs to since her betrothed is a doctor."

"She should get you in."

"In where?" she asked with a confused expression.

"Into the magazine. You could model too."

She gave me a serious expression. "I'm five feet tall."

"So? Isn't Tom Cruise the same height? But you can never tell on screen."

She tried not to laugh. "I'm not model material."

"Bullshit," I blurted. "Look at you." I peered into the water.

She kicked my shin. "Watch it, man."

I moved away, a slight smirk on my lips. "We're friends. I'll show you mine if you show me yours."

"Nope."

I stared at her, the area above water. She had petite rounded shoulders that led to a slender neck. Her skin was flawless and unblemished. I stared at it and wondered how her skin would taste. I fantasized about her wrapping her legs around my waist while I kissed her hard on the mouth.

58

My cock twitched and grew, and I knew I needed to keep my cool.

Her face was the best part. She was beautiful in a classic way. I'd always been into brunettes before Alexia, but after she left, my attraction stuck to blondes. And Harper was an exceptional beauty. Her high cheekbones led to sparkling blue eyes. They shined by their own light and were hypnotic. I'd never been attracted to a girl like this before. I usually had to force it. But these feelings toward Harper were giving me hope. If I was into her, then that meant I was finally letting go of the past. Maybe I could move on and start picking up girls like I wanted to. Now I wouldn't have to pretend to be a playboy. I could actually just be one.

Without my knowledge, my body moved closer to hers. My legs had their own mind, and they were in league with my throbbing cock. I came closer to her then gripped her waist. Then I pressed my mouth to hers.

Her lips were immobile and lifeless. But they kissed me back, just for a moment. And in the span of those heartbeats, I felt electricity course through me like never before. The hair on the back of my neck stood on end and I felt a distant shiver move down my spine. Her lips were soft and full like I expected. Her tits pressed against my chest and they felt amazing, even under the water.

She pushed me back. "What the hell are you doing?"

The hot moment was ruined. I tried to gather my wits but I was a little confused. I kissed her without thinking about it, and as soon as I did, I was lost.

"Earth to Troy!"

My eyes found hers. "Sorry. You're really hot."

She rolled her eyes and sighed at the same time. "So you just try to make out with me?"

"I wasn't thinking, honestly. It was like I went into a trance."

"Yeah right," she said. "That was why you tried to get me to skinny dip."

"It really wasn't."

"Whatever," she said. "Just don't do it again."

"Are you sure?" I asked. "Because that kiss was pretty hot."

"Hot or not, we're just friends."

"Who kiss?" I asked hopefully.

"Just friends. Period."

"Who do other things...?"

She shot me a glare. "Like you could do other things if you tried."

"So, is kissing still on the table?"

She splashed me. "Start thinking with the head on your shoulders and not the one between your legs."

"Uh, they're thinking the same thing regardless."

She growled. "Close your eyes and turn around."

"Come on, you liked that kiss too."

"No, I didn't," she argued.

"You're such a liar."

"Am not!"

"You kissed me back for like thirty seconds before you pushed me off. Explain that!"

She glared at me again but remained quiet.

"That's what I thought."

"I was just in shock."

"Because I'm an awesome kisser."

"You're so full of yourself."

"Hey, you're an awesome kisser too. Your lips taste like honey."

She didn't get out of the pool. "Is this how you hit on all girls? Because you need to step up your game."

"I've never skinny-dipped with someone before," I said honestly. "And I've never gone into a trance like that before. It was like I had no control over anything I did."

"Whatever, Troy."

"Let's make out again."

She splashed me in the face. "The moment is over. Let's move on."

I growled just the way she had.

"Now turn around and close your eyes."

"Okay, fine." I turned around and didn't look.

"You better not peek."

"I didn't peek when you got in so why would I peak now?"

"Because you're horny."

She had a point. "I won't, okay?"

"You're such a liar."

"Does it really matter if I see you?" I asked.

"Yes," she said firmly.

"Well, hurry up before I get tired of standing here."

The water moved as she got out and then I heard the sound of drops hitting the pavement.

Man, I really want to look. I only got a glimpse of her in the water but I couldn't really see anything. But her chest felt amazing when it was pressed to mine. She was probably a B or C cup.

Her feet padded against the concrete as she walked to the towel.

Now or never. I discreetly glanced over my shoulder.

Fuck, she was fine. She had a perky ass, tiny waist, and perfect tits. I wanted to shove my fist in my mouth so I wouldn't yell.

"Troy!"

I turned back around. "What?"

"You're such a jerk." I heard her wrap a towel around her body.

I started to get out of the pool. "Look, I tried not to."

She rolled her eyes.

"But you're just so beautiful that I couldn't."

"You're unbelievable."

"I'll make it fair." I walked out of the pool with my hard dick on display. "Full frontal nudity."

She looked down and stared at my length for a heartbeat. Then she tossed me a towel. "Looks like we're even."

"So...are you sure you don't want to make out again?" I wrapped my towel around my waist.

"It's not *that* impressive, Troy."

I gave her a cocky smirk. "Liar."

She grabbed her clothes from the concrete. "I'm going to change in the bathroom."

"You need help, Perfect Ten?"

"No, thank you, Eight Inches."

"Is that my nickname?" I asked. "I like it."

She walked inside the house without responding.

***

We sat in silence on the drive. The radio was on low in the background. Harper looked out the window and didn't make conversation with me once.

"Mad at me?" I asked.

"What do you think?" she asked coldly.

I didn't want to be on bad terms with her. "Take it as a compliment."

"Oh, I feel better now," she said sarcastically.

I sighed, hating myself for messing up the friendship we just started to have. "Want to know something honest about me?" Being open with her seemed to gain her confidence. Hopefully, it would work again.

"I'm listening..."

"I'm trusting you not to tell Rhett, and especially not Aspen."

"Well, if I'm as trustworthy as you are, then you're in for a surprise."

"Harper." My voice came out serious. "I know I can trust you."

She finally turned her head my way.

"You were right about me and all the girls—or lack of girls."

"Yeah?" she asked.

"The truth is, I haven't been with anyone in a really long time."

She stared at me in silence, heartbeats of time passing.

"I just...I don't want to."

"Why?" she asked quietly.

"I'm not really sure, to be honest. I know I have intimacy issues. It's hard for me to be open with someone. Any time conversations become too serious, I say something stupid and ruin it. And opening myself to someone in that way...it's just too difficult for me no matter how meaningless it is."

"It didn't seem like you had a problem in the pool," she noted.

"I know." I swallowed the lump in my throat. "And that gives me hope."

"Hope that what?" she whispered.

"That I'm finally getting better and I can start sleeping around again. You know, be a normal guy."

"Why do you have to sleep around?" she asked. "Why can't you just date and have another relationship?"

"No," I blurted. "Never. I'll never do that again."

She looked out the window.

"That was a mistake and I'll never do it again."

"Just because one woman didn't value you doesn't mean another one won't. You're very sweet, Troy. I think there are a lot of great qualities in you, and if you gave someone the opportunity to love you they would."

Her words meant nothing to me so I didn't comment on them. "I'm sorry if I pissed you off and crossed the line. I call you a Perfect Ten because I really think you're a Perfect Ten. Obviously, I'm very much attracted to you."

"Do you want to sleep with me?" she asked bluntly.

"Theoretically, yes. In reality, no."

"Can you explain that?" she asked calmly.

"You're hot. Obviously, I'd fuck you. But you're Aspen's friend, whose Rhett's woman. It would be a really bad idea and I don't want to make things complicated for Rhett. If I slept with you and never called again, it would make things tense."

"I'm so glad my feelings were put into consideration..."

"And that too," I said quickly. "My point is, I'm sorry for my behavior and I would really like to be friends. I'll keep my lips to myself."

"And your junk in your pants." There was a slight smile on her lips so I knew she wasn't mad.

I turned to her. "So, we're cool? Because I think you're really awesome and I don't want to lose this friendship because my dick likes you too much."

She released a faint laugh. "A lot of dicks like me."

"I believe it. So?"

"I would love to be your friend, Troy."

"Sweet." I nudged her in the side playfully.

She nudged me back. "Are we going to be those awkward friends that inappropriately touch each other after every pun and joke?"

I nudged her again. "I hope so."

Harper

"What do you think?" I stood in front of the mocha colored leather sofa. "I can get a really good deal on it plus my discount. It's practically a steal."

He walked around the couch then sat on it. He reclined then put his hands behind his head. Then his eyes closed and he sat absolutely still for several moments. When his breathing became deep and steady, I knew something was off.

"Wake up, Troy."

He stirred then blinked his eyes quickly. "Yep. This couch will do."

I tried not to laugh. "It's in your budget?"

"Yep." He put the recliner down then got up. He moved his fingers through his hair like he just woke up. He was naturally sexy without even trying, and a group of passing girls noticed the same thing I noticed. Kissing him was pretty terrific. I wasn't going to deny it—except to him.

"Then let's do it." We walked to the counter and purchased the couch. The other knickknacks were already at the house. I just had to do the final decorating but I didn't want to start until the big things were in the house, like the couches, beds, and rugs.

Troy put everything on a credit card and we walked out of the store.

"Everything is finally ready," I said with excitement. "Now I just need to set up."

"I can help," he said. "You want to go there now?"

"No, it's okay," I said immediately. "It's what you're paying me to do."

"I don't mind helping," he said immediately. "Unless you're scared to be alone with me." He nudged me awkwardly in the side.

"Yes, you caught me," I said sarcastically.

"Come on," he said. "We'll make lunch and make a day out of it. Then we'll hit the beach."

I gave him a pissed look.

"In our swimsuits, of course," he said with a laugh.

"Okay, that's better."

***

There were stacks of boxes everywhere. I had a lot to do and so little time. It was probably a blessing in disguise that Troy offered to help. He had the muscle and size to move tables and chairs. And he could reach high places with his height. My short stature limited my mobility sometimes.

"Damn, you bought a lot of shit." He walked around the boxes and had to jump over a few.

"But this place will look amazing."

"It better." He opened a random box. "I don't know where any of this stuff goes..."

"Just take care of the big stuff."

"Like?"

"The table." I pointed to the big box. "You have tools, right?"

"Do I look like a construction worker to you?"

"No. But you don't look stupid either."

"I have a screwdriver."

"That should be enough."

We worked in comfortable silence. He assembled the large furniture while I decorated the house with paintings and assembled lamps on the different end tables. Within hours, the place started to look brand new.

Troy got hot so he took off his t-shirt. He didn't look at me when he did, lost in his own world.

But I looked at him and noticed the chiseled muscles of his chest and stomach. He clearly hit the gym and often. He had a small build like a soccer player, but he was ripped in the arms, chest, and stomach. I'd be lying if I said I wasn't attracted to Troy. But I didn't want to date him or sleep with him. I didn't mind fooling around with different men, but Troy was off limits. Besides, he'd become a good friend recently and I liked having him around. I didn't want to give him a reason to leave.

By the later afternoon, we were only about halfway done.

Troy wiped the sweat from his forehead then leaned against the wall. "I think we should call it a day and come back some other time."

I was tired too. "Yeah, maybe."

"There's not much daylight left. If we hit the beach we should do it now."

"But let's eat first."

He snapped his fingers then pointed at me. "Good call." He walked into his kitchen and searched the pantry. "PB&J okay?"

"That sounds perfect to me."

He pulled out the bread and made two sandwiches. He handed me one before he sat on the counter and ate his. Like he was in a daze, he stared at an empty spot on the wall, clearly exhausted.

I ate slowly, almost too tired to do that.

"Can I ask you something?" He turned his gaze back to me.

"I suppose."

"Did you not feel anything when you kissed me?"

Why was he asking? "What does it matter?"

"Because I felt something. I find it hard to believe you didn't."

I kept eating then averted my gaze, trying to seem indifferent.

He gave me that smirk I'd come to love. It meant he had me and he knew it. "Your lack of response tells me all I need to know."

"Look, kissing a hot naked guy in a pool would make anyone feel that way," I said defensively.

"You think I'm hot?" His smile widened.

"No, I'm just saying..."

"Nope, you said it." He fist-pounded the air. "Perfect Ten thinks Eight Inches is hot."

"We sound like porn stars."

He laughed. "That's pretty hot. Maybe we should make one together." He winked at me.

"What happened to just being friends?"

"We are just friends. That doesn't mean we can't enjoy making out." He finished his sandwich but remained on the counter. "And I like teasing you. Your cheeks turn red and it's really cute."

"Cute?" I asked.

"Yeah."

"That's the first time I heard you use that word."

"Well, you're the first cute thing I've seen." He jumped off the counter then headed to the patio. "We're heading to the beach or what?"

"I need to change."

"Or you could change out here." He wiggled his eyebrows then walked out. "I'll be at the beach."

I rolled my eyes even though he couldn't see me then changed into my purple bikini. Then I walked across the sand to where Troy lay on two beach towels. He wore swim trunks without a shirt.

I sat beside him then put on my sunglasses.

Troy whistled loudly. "Purple is a good color on you."

"Thank you." *Would it be vain for me to say I liked it when he complimented me?*

He propped himself on his elbows and looked out to sea. It was a perfect day and a cloudless sky. The ocean was a bright blue just like the heavens, and the sun took up the sky.

"It's a nice day."

"It is," he agreed. He stared at the beach before he turned back to me. Then he looked away again.

"What?" I asked.

"I didn't say anything." He squinted his eyes because of the sun but he still looked hot when he did it.

"Then why did you look at me?"

"Friends or not, you're hot. I like to look at you."

"Do you ever censor your thoughts?

"No," he said. "I'm a very honest person. That might be annoying sometimes but at least you know what you're getting from me. There's never any room for misinterpretation."

"I guess that's true."

"You, on the other hand, I never know what you're thinking." He leaned toward me. "And I'd give anything to know."

"You seem to think my unknown thoughts are interesting."

"I'm sure they are."

"Not really," I said.

"How about we both be brutally honest with each other from now on?" he asked. He lay on his back and rested his hands behind his head.

"Why?" I rested my elbows on my knees and dug my toes into the sand.

"Because that's what real friends do. They're honest with each other."

"A hundred percent?" I asked.

"Aren't you that way with Aspen?"

"Not a hundred percent. Are you that way with Rhett?"

"No."

"Then why should we be that way?"

He shrugged. "Because I like you a lot, Harper."

I lay back and rested one hand on my stomach. My hair cascaded around me and the sun felt warm on my skin. "Why do you like me so much?"

"Well, you're really cool. But you're also a little pessimistic. You know, you aren't bubbly and talking about rainbows and unicorns all the time. It's refreshing. I hate it when people are too over-the-top happy."

"That makes sense. So, you like me because I'm depressing?"

"Depressing is too strong of a word. Normal is better."

I closed my eyes and felt the sun beat into me. There was a slight breeze so I wasn't too warm.

"So, honesty from now on?"

"Sure."

"Cool," he said. "So, are you attracted to me?"

He didn't waste any time. "I just said you were hot a few minutes ago, didn't I?"

"So, you meant it?"

I sighed. "Troy, would you be an escort if you weren't extremely attractive?"

"Being attractive is subjective," he said. "My friends will point out girls who they think are perfect tens and they look like shit."

I released a laugh. "Well, that's mean."

"I'm just being honest like I said I would be."

"Yeah..."

"So?" he pressed.

"So what?"

"You think I'm hot?"

"Why do you want to know?" I countered. I adjusted my sunglasses on the bridge of my nose.

"Because I want to know if you're just as attracted to me as I am to you."

So, he was being completely honest. "Yes."

A stupid grin stretched his face. "Awesome."

I kept my eyes closed and enjoyed the sun.

"So, you did like kissing me?"

I sighed. "Troy, why are you asking all these questions if all we'll ever be is friends?"

"Because I'm curious—very curious."

"Fine," I said with a sigh. "I'm going to save you some time and tell you everything you might ask about."

"I'm intrigued." He propped himself on his elbows again.

"I've been attracted to you since the moment I saw you. But since you're an escort, I'll never be interested in dating you. Aspen is a trusting person because she is sweet and...fucking weird...but I'm not like that. I'm more of the jealous type. If I had a boyfriend, I don't want him touching anyone but me.

"When we kissed, I felt something. It was hot, and you're a great kisser. I love your body, and I even love the stupid smile you always make, like the one you're making right now."

His grin stretched wider.

"I'd sleep with you if there wasn't obvious complications. But honestly, I like having you as a friend anyway so it works out."

He processed my words for a long time. "So, why wouldn't you kiss me again?"

I shrugged. "The moment was gone."

"Would you want to kiss me again?"

This was going to dangerous territory. "I don't think it's a good idea."

He stared at the incoming waves. "Why don't we be friends with benefits?"

"I thought you weren't sleeping around anymore."

"Well, that's the thing," he said. "I'd like to try. You're the first girl I've been this attracted to in a really long time. What if we...fool around? We won't tell anyone. It'll be our secret."

That was tempting. "What's your end game?"

"To finally move on and be with other women."

I thought about the story he told me about his ex. "You aren't over her, are you?"

He quickly looked away like he was ashamed. There was nowhere for him to hide. He was the one who wanted to be honest. Now he had to face the music. "I...I'm not sure. But I don't think I am." His voice came out weak, like it took all his strength to speak. "Does that bother you?"

"No. As long as you're honest about it."

He sighed then lay back down. "I hate myself for feeling this way...she won't go away no matter what I do. I'm doomed to suffer this forever. I'm so pathetic."

I rested my hand on his arm. "That doesn't make you pathetic."

"She left me for some other guy over a year ago," he said quietly. "You'd think I'd be over it by now. I had the ring and everything...then she left." His voice was full of emotion. He sounded like a completely different person.

"Its her loss, Troy. You're an amazing guy, despite all your attempts to hide it. It may not seem like it but it's the best thing that ever happened to you. You'll realize that someday."

"Maybe...maybe not."

I moved close to him and rubbed his shoulder. "So, you want me to help you get over her?"

"Yes." His voice was full of shame.

"Well, there's something I want in return."

"Name it."

"I want you to escort me."

He turned to me, confusion in his eyes. "Why?"

"My sister's wedding is going to be a disaster. I'll be a talking point for everyone there. But if they think I have a serious boyfriend, they'll stop riding my ass."

He nodded. "Well, I can't accept payment for it. Since we're sleeping together...we just can't. But I'll gladly do it privately."

"Yeah?" I asked with a spurt of joy.

"Yeah. I'll make everyone think I'm more in love with you than your sister's fiancé is with your sister."

"Well, that's impossible."

"Psh," he said. "I've been doing this for years. Leave it to me."

"Then it looks like we have a deal." I extended my hand to shake his.

He looked at it but didn't take it. Instead, he nudged me in the side. "Deal."

***

I arrived at the restaurant last, unfortunately. My family was already seated at a table, and I did my best to walk with grace as I approached them. Wearing a fake smile and doing my best to seem pleased to be there, I sat down and said quick hellos to everyone. "Sorry, I'm late."

"It's okay," Kara said. "We know things are hectic right now."

"Thanks," I said.

"But you could have called ahead," Mom said.

I clenched my menu but didn't say anything. *Never hit your mom.*

Mom and Kara finished their conversation about the centerpieces for the wedding. I wasn't sure why they were planning ahead so early but that was their own prerogative.

"Well, we actually didn't ask you guys to meet us here to discuss centerpieces..." Kara turned to Sebastian with a smile on her face. It was a look of encouragement, of excitement.

"Then what's your news?" Mom asked. "Did you find a dress?"

"No..." Kara was practically squirming in her seat.

Just spit it out already.

Sebastian watched her with affection in his eyes.

No one would ever look at me like that.

Kara took Sebastian's hand. "We're having a baby!" She smiled wide and watched my parents' reactions.

Oh shit, she was having a baby? Mom and Dad would be pissed. They wouldn't even pay for the wedding if Kara were knocked up out of wedlock. They would disown me immediately if they thought I was pregnant. I watched my parents, waiting for the explosion.

"That's wonderful!" Mom covered her mouth and gasped.

What?

"We're going to be grandparents, dear," Dad said.

Say what?

"I knew you would be supportive," Kara said. "Sebastian and I are so excited. Obviously, it's earlier than we planned but that doesn't mean we aren't thrilled about it."

"I'm very thrilled about it." Sebastian gave her a quick kiss and looked into her eyes with fondness.

This better be a fucking joke.

My parents got up and hugs were exchanged. I finally forced myself out of my seat and hugged Kara. "Congratulations." I was happy for my sister but I was pissed that my parents didn't hold Kara to the same standards they held me. She could do no wrong, but I was judged for every little thing. "How far along are you?"

"About a month," she said. "Only eight more to go."

Sebastian hugged me. "You're going to be an aunt."

"I am," I said. "Congratulations."

"Thank you." He returned to Kara's side like a magnet.

When we sat down again, the weight of the situation hit me. Now my sister was getting married and having a baby. My mom would be on my ass a million times harder. *Geez...*

"So, are you still having the wedding next summer?" Mom asked.

"Well, I don't want to be a cow when we get married," Kara said.

Sebastian shook his head. "You would never look like a cow."

Mom smiled at him. "You found yourself a good husband, Kara."

I was going to need Troy a little earlier than I planned.

"So, we want to get married in a month." Kara grinned but it wasn't genuine. It was more of a cringe than anything else.

Sebastian cleared his throat. "The reason being, we want to get married in Hawaii and she can't fly past her first trimester. And we want to have a nice honeymoon before the morning sickness arrives."

A month? That just wasn't doable.

"We know it's short notice but it's what we want," Kara said firmly.

Now Mom and Dad would explode. This was too much, too fast. And they were old-fashioned.

"We think it's great," Dad said. "If a wedding in paradise is what you want, we'll make it happen."

My jaw was on the floor.

'Thank you, Daddy." Kara rested her hand on his.

So, she gets knocked up and gets a dream wedding? And I'm the loser of the family? I wanted to scream.

Kara turned to me. "We have a lot of planning to do."

I put on a fake smile. "Yeah, we'll make it through." How were we supposed to plan a wedding that far away? In a month? This was crazy.

"I'm so glad one of my daughters is getting married and starting a family," Mom said. "It might be the only one."

She did not just go there. I turned my wide eyes on her.

Kara cringed, like she felt my pain at the insult.

"Well, I'm bringing my boyfriend to the wedding. Perhaps we'll get some wedding tips while we're there."

That came out of my mouth like an uncontrollable waterfall. I wasn't thinking. I was just mad.

Everyone turned my way.

"Boyfriend?" Mom asked. "Last time we spoke, you told me you weren't seeing anyone."

"I didn't want to talk about it at the time," I lied. "Kara just got engaged. I didn't want to steal her thunder." It was the only thing I could come up with. In reality, Mom asked about my personal life before Sebastian proposed. So...that didn't make sense. But I doubt anyone would realize it.

Mom looked at me in a new way, like she actually liked me. "That's wonderful, honey. Is it serious?"

"Super, duper serious," I blurted. "Like, we're serious." I knew I sounded stupid but I couldn't control my tongue.

"I'm so happy for you," Kara said. "What's he like?"

Think quickly. "His name is Troy. He's gorgeous." *What did he do for a living?* "He owns an online dating company and is worth a shit ton of money." That wasn't totally true but it would work. "And...we're madly in love."

"Wow." Kara couldn't see past my lies. "That's amazing, Harper. I can't wait to meet him."

"Invite him to dinner this weekend," Mom said. "To the house."

That quickly? I thought I would spare myself some time. "I'll let him know."

"That's great," Dad said to Mom. "Maybe both of our girls will be gone from the nest too."

Gone from the nest? I've been living on my own for seven years...and never once did I ask them for money. I wasn't sure why Kara asked them to pay for her wedding.

She and Sebastian should pay for it themselves if they wanted to have a ridiculous wedding in paradise. But that was just me.

My parents were in a festive mood. They were laughing and drinking their wine like water.

Was me finding a boyfriend that important? Was the fact I was happy on my own irrelevant? None of my accomplishments mattered to them. All they cared about was putting a ring on my finger—like that would solve all my problems.

***

Troy picked up on the first ring. "Hey, Perfect Ten. Ready to get down and dirty?"

I rolled my eyes even though he couldn't see me. "I have a crisis on my hands and I need to talk."

His playfulness evaporated, replaced by seriousness. "Are you okay? Where are you?"

"I'm fine. Where are you?"

"At home."

"Can I come over?"

"Of course," he said. "I'll text you the address."

"Okay." I hung up then headed to his apartment. I'd never been there before, just his beach house. As I navigated to it on my phone, I realized it was in a nice district of the city. Since he bought a beach house, I already assumed he was wealthy, but it still surprised me.

As soon as I got to the door, he opened it without waiting for me to knock.

"You okay?" he asked immediately. He wore jeans and a t-shirt, looking hot like usual.

"I'm okay. I'm not hurt or anything."

"Come inside and talk to me." His arm moved around my waist and he chauffeured me inside.

I liked having his hand on my waist. It was a feeling I'd never felt before.

He moved me to the couch and gave me his full attention. "What's up?"

"My sister is having a damn baby."

A blank expression came over his face. "And that's bad because..."

"She's not married."

Now he became confused. "So, you agree to sleep with me so I can move on, but you're going to judge her for having a baby out of wedlock? I got to say, that's pretty hypocritical."

"No." I waved him away. "That's not what I'm mad about."

"Then you need to explain."

"She's getting married in a month because she doesn't want to show in her dress," I explained. "Then my mom made a bitchy comment about only marrying off one daughter so I blurted out that you and I were super serious and madly in love and crap."

He shrugged. "Well, that's what we agreed on."

"But they want to meet you this weekend," I argued. "I just wanted you around for the wedding."

He shrugged again. "I'll do it as long as you need me. I don't mind."

"I'm a terrible liar. I don't think I can be convincing that long."

"Well, I'm a great liar," he said. "I'll take care of it."

"How admirable," I said sarcastically.

"Harper, just chill."

I took a deep breath. "You're right. I'm overreacting right now. I just...this is all happening so fast. And the wedding is in Hawaii."

"Really?" he asked. "That sounds fun."

"You don't mind taking a weekend off of work?"

"Not at all," he said. "You and I will have a good time." He patted my hand. "Don't worry about it. Everything will be okay."

I nodded. "You're right. I went bat-shit crazy there."

"When you called I thought you were mugged or something. I was terrified."

"Sorry," I said. "I didn't mean to scare you."

"It's okay," he said. "Just don't do it again."

"Deal."

He leaned back into the couch and relaxed. "You want to go get a burger?"

"A burger?"

"From that diner?" he asked. "Where we ran into each other?"

"That does sound awesome."

He smiled, and it was different than all the other ones he gave me. "Then let's go."

***

We took our seats then ordered our food.

Troy sat across from me, his shoulders looking broad in his shirt. We hadn't talked about our relationship since the beach house. We agreed to be friends with benefits but no fooling around had actually taken place. I wasn't in a hurry and neither was he. But I was looking forward to it. He had a nice package and a nice kiss. I'm sure everything else would be good too. And I cared about him—more than I thought I would even though he was a jerk sometimes.

"Why do your parents care so much about you being married off anyway?" he asked. "Isn't it more impressive that their daughter is financially and emotionally capable of being alone rather than needing someone to fill that void? That's how I would feel at least. Actually, if I had a daughter, I would want her to be alone forever."

I laughed because the idea of Troy having kids was hilarious.

"What?" he asked.

"I just can't picture you with kids."

"Neither can I," he admitted. "And none of them have come up unexpectedly." He knocked on the wood of the table.

"I'm not sure if I want kids either."

"Really?" He looked at me with surprise in his eyes. "Why is that?"

I shrugged. "Maybe when I find the right guy I'll feel differently. But I'm so busy with work that I just can't picture it. But then again, I can't picture myself finding the right guy to fall in love with."

"What's your idea of the right guy?" he asked.

"Why?" I stared at him suspiciously.

"I'm just curious. I thought I was the right guy for Alexia but she left anyway." There was no bitterness in his eyes, just calm acceptance.

"Well, first of all, he needs to be hot."

He nodded. "Of course."

"He needs to make me laugh."

"Absolutely."

"And...?"

"What else?" he asked.

"He's got to be my best friend too."

"Well, that doesn't sound unrealistic," he said. "You can find that guy anywhere on the street."

"You would think," I said sadly. "I've dated a lot and met interesting people but...whatever spark that needs to be there is just not there. There's always something about them I don't like."

"You're picky," he said. "That's good. I hate 'I love you' whores or girls who will be with anyone who gives them the eye. The only girl worth waiting for is the girl who doesn't wait for anyone."

I cocked my head to the side, more surprised with him. "For being against relationships, you speak highly of them."

"No, I don't," he said. "I'm just expressing the fact that women should be choosy with men. Women are the better-looking sex so they have all the power. They should use that to their advantage. I hate seeing chicks at parties that go to bed with any guy just because they have enough liquor in their system. And you're drop dead gorgeous, Harper. You shouldn't be with anyone unless they're absolutely perfect."

"You speak so highly of me," I said quietly.

"I think the world of you," he said seriously. "You're pretty, you're smart, you're successful, and you don't put up with bullshit. You got all the ingredients to make a perfect woman."

"But I'm not the perfect woman to you."

He shrugged. "But that's only because I don't believe in such a thing—at least anymore."

It was a pity this girl ruined him so much. He could be the perfect man if he wanted to be. But she permanently scarred him and made him a ghost of a man. He was too scared of women and relationships. Hopefully, he would change his mind someday. "That makes me sad."

He turned serious. "Don't feel bad for me. I just had poor taste in women."

"Just because she left you doesn't mean she didn't love you before—"

He held up his hand. "I don't want to talk about her."

I dropped the subject.

The food arrived and that made the atmosphere less awkward. He grabbed his burger and took large bites. I picked at my fries and loved the taste of the grease. The silence stretched for a long time but it wasn't uncomfortable. Troy and I were fairly comfortable with each other at this point.

"I want to talk about our arrangement." He was serious, like he was running a business conference that had a lot of money on the line.

"Okay."

"I really care about you and I think you're amazing."

It was a really sweet thing to say and I didn't expect it out of his mouth.

"And I don't want to hurt you. I need you to understand that this arrangement will never lead to a relationship or love. I will never feel that way, and please don't think you have the power to change me. You don't, and no girl does. I need you to understand this completely. If not, I can't go through with it. If you've changed your mind, that's fine. I will still help you out with your family because you're my friend. So don't feel obligated to go through with it."

"I don't expect you to feel anything romantic toward me or have deep feelings. But I do hope you rethink your view on relationships and try again—someday."

"I never will," he said simply. "Please don't try to change my mind."

I looked down at my plate of fries.

"And you can't feel anything for me. I'll never return those feelings and it will only hurt you."

"Troy, don't worry about that," I said. "That won't happen."

"May I ask why?"

"You're not Mr. Right. If you were, I would have known from the beginning. They say you know someone is the one the moment you meet. It doesn't take longer than a conversation. And we've had several conversations about different things. It's not you, Troy."

"Okay," he said with a nod. "Then let me ask you something. What do you get out of this?"

"Uh, you're hot. A girl has needs too."

That typical grin broke out on his face. "Good answer."

"And this is to remain a secret. Neither one of us can tell anyone."

"Consider it done," he said. "Are we monogamous?"

"Yes." Sleeping with one guy I didn't love was slutty enough. And I didn't have a long line of guys waiting for a chance to be with me.

"Good. It looks like we have an agreement."

"I think so."

We kept eating.

Troy finished his burger than moved onto his fries. "Nervous?"

"No. You?"

"Are we still being completely honest with each other?" he asked.

"Always."

"Then yes."

Troy hadn't been active in his personal life so I wasn't surprised if he was nervous. When we were finally alone together it might be awkward. Neither one of us might know what to do. Or it could fall naturally into place. I didn't have a clue.

The bill came and Troy paid for it. "Ready to head back to my place?"

When I remembered the way that kiss felt, excitement coursed through me. "Yes."

***

We entered his apartment and I looked around. I was pleased to see that it was similar to the style of his beach house. I did a good job understanding what he wanted and making it a home he could feel comfortable with.

I tossed my purse on the couch then turned to him.

He came close to me, his eyes moving to my lips. "Want to know a secret?"

"Sure."

"I looked in the water a few times when we were skinny dipping."

"Is that supposed to surprise me?" I asked.

A grin stretched his face, and it somehow always made me feel warm. "But I didn't see much. But when I did take a peek when I wasn't supposed to...wow. I've been thinking about it ever since."

"What did you like?"

"Everything," he blurted.

"I liked what I saw too," I admitted.

"Well, eight inches is pretty impressive..."

"I knew you liked it." That cocky grin was on his face. He cornered me against the couch and rested his hands on either side of me. I was blocked in but I didn't mind being unable to get away. He pressed his forehead to mine and stared down at me.

My hands moved to his arms, exploring the muscle I'd thought about for a long time. They felt good on my fingers, strong and powerful. My hands moved across the skin and I was surprised how soft he was.

Troy's hands moved slightly up my shirt to my hips. "If you want me to stop, just tell me." His voice came out quiet and gentle.

"I know."

"You don't owe me anything."

I stared at his lips and felt his warm breath fall on my skin. "Shut up and kiss me already."

A deep chuckle came from deep in his throat. "Perfect Ten is bossy..." He leaned in the rest of the way and pressed his lips gently against mine. The kiss wasn't aggressive like before. He took his time, like he had the rest of his life to kiss me. One hand slowly moved up my shoulder and neck until it settled in my hair. He fists it like he needed it to survive. Then the kiss deepened.

Like last time, the sparks flew. My lips felt warm every time they touched his, and I forgot about everything around me when our bodies were combined. He knew exactly how to move his mouth, to feel my lips completely rather than move randomly. Then when his tongue entered my mouth, a quiet gasp escaped involuntarily.

Troy was amazing.

He seemed to feel the same chemistry because he gripped me tighter. He had a firm hold on me, like he wasn't going to let me get away even if I asked him to stop. His hand dug further into my hair, like he owned it and the rest of me.

He pressed into me harder and circled my waist with one arm. He pulled me close, my boobs pressed against his chest. He suddenly ended our kiss then moved his lips to my neck. His hand tugged on my hair, forcing my head back, and his soft lips moved to the exposed skin. He kissed me like a vampire sucking blood. His tongue moved around, tasting me. Then he slowly inched to my ear, his warm breaths amplified due to the proximity. "Gorgeous." That was all he said. Then he moved back to my lips and kissed me harder than before, with desperation and need.

He suddenly picked me up and pulled me to his chest. My legs automatically wrapped around his waist like they had a mind of their own. I squeezed his hips, telling him I was excited without the use of words. Still kissing me like a man who lived a week in the desert without water, he guided me to his bed. He gently laid me down and moved over me at the same time, like he'd done it a thousand times.

My legs tightened around his waist and my hands moved up his shirt, feeling every groove and definition of muscle. He was thin, but there was no fat on his body. He was all muscle and strength. I loved feeling every groove and valley. I felt like I was feeling a sculpture, with infinite details in every line and molding. I suddenly gripped his shoulders and held on, like he was going to take me to a place where I'd lose all control.

Troy lifted up my shirt to the area beneath my breasts then moved down. His lips found my stomach and he kissed the area. He moved to each hip and devoured the skin. His tongue danced around my body, sampling every place he could reach. Then he moved back up until he found my lips again.

My hand moved to his shirt, eager to see his naked body pressed to mine.

But he grabbed my hand and pinned it above my head. "I really love kissing you. Can we just do that tonight?"

I was disappointed because I was eager to feel him inside me. The chemistry between us was right and I wanted to revel in a night of pleasure. But if that's what he wanted, that's what he would get. He was an amazing kisser anyway so I didn't mind. There really was no rush.

Gorgeous Consort

Rhett

Harper was something.

She was the best kisser I've ever had. She did this sexy thing with her tongue and it sent chills down my spine. The endless curves and valleys of that perfect body made me harder than a rock. And I just loved being with her.

I could be myself with her and not hide anymore. Any other time I was out, I had to pretend I was looking for new pussy and that I was some macho jerk. But with her, I could just admit I wasn't everything I pretended to be. She understood who I really was. And letting my walls down was the nicest feeling in the world.

I couldn't have sex with her in the moment. I just wasn't ready to. It had to be right, and there was no point in rushing it when I couldn't perform at my best. Her pleasure was important to me, and I wanted to give her a reason to enjoy this arrangement as much as I did. She didn't seem to mind that I hit the brakes on the drive. She was patient with me, just like a friend should be.

Nate's production was tonight, and of course, I was going. That guy needed as much support as possible. He was going through a hard time, dealing with the fact he may lose his parents forever. No one should have to go through that. Life was too short to push away family over something so idiotic.

I made a stop before I headed to the theatre. I headed to the front door of the apartment then knocked. For the fact I was risking my neck, I didn't feel that terrified. It was something I had to do.

Nate's father opened the door, his wife just behind him. Loathing was in his eyes while he looked at me. It was clear he viewed me as pigeon vomit on the sidewalk. Despise and disdain was etched into every line of his face.

Like I gave a damn.

I pulled out the two tickets. "Nate's show is tonight. It would mean a lot to him if you came."

His father was silent for so long I didn't think he would speak.

"You're the one missing out on things," I said. "He's yours son, whether he loves men or women, and he's incredibly brave for being himself in a society that may not fully accept him. As a father your job is to love your child unconditionally. You're failing at that—miserably."

He took a step forward, his shoulders squared for battle. "What did you say to me?"

"You heard me—clearly. If you want to solve this debate with violence, fine. But I have to warn you, I'll kick your ass and I'd rather not. It gives me no satisfaction beating up an old man." I tossed the tickets on the ground. "I sincerely hope you change your mind. Nate is a good kid. It's sad that you don't see that." I walked away without looking back, knowing they wouldn't show up despite my efforts to convince them. If anything, I only provoked them more.

***

Kyle stood outside the theatre and checked his Rolex, wondering where I was.

"Sorry I'm late." I reached him then handed the ticket over.

"You're always late," he said. "I stopped expecting otherwise." He insulted me but grinned at the same time. He was the same height as me, and we had features that were so similar we looked like twins. It was hard to believe my brother was two years older than me.

"Where's Mark?" I asked.

"He's sick," he said sadly. "Came down with something."

"Oh, sorry to hear that."

"He'll make it through," Kyle said. "He can be a pussy about it sometimes."

I laughed. "What a sweet way to talk about your betrothed."

He shrugged. "Hey, when it's true I'm not going to deny it. So, how'd it go with your friend's parents?"

I shook my head. "Somehow, I made the situation worse. They actually want to murder me."

He released a sigh. "Sometimes people are so set in their ways that they'll never change. I suggest you just let it go."

"But it's such a stupid reason to disown your son. What does it matter what hole he sticks his dick in? Shit, I've fucked tons of girls in the ass."

He laughed. "Classy..."

94

"I'm just saying."

"I'm sure your friend appreciates all of this but sometimes you just have to admit when the battle is over. It doesn't mean you lost the war." Kyle was a lot more mature than I was. After the things he'd been through, he naturally aged quicker than most people. He balanced me and the idiotic things I would say.

We handed our tickets over then filed inside the theatre. The design of chairs and classic ceiling gave the place an artistic look. It was beautiful and elegant. It reminded me of Harper and her design abilities. She really had a knack for it, and she was clearly passionate about it.

"Anything new with your personal life?" Kyle asked as he sat beside me. "Or are you still pretending to be something you aren't?" Kyle was one of the few people I trusted. Since he was my brother and confided something so personal to me, that he was gay, I reciprocated back. I was the first person he admitted the truth to, and that meant a lot to me.

"Well...there's this girl."

He turned to me, and his eyes widened in interest. A smile broke out on his face. "Yeah?" Happiness was clear in his eyes. "Tell me about her."

"She's blonde, C-cup, and has gorgeous legs."

He narrowed his eyes. "Troy, come on." He never let me get away with my sleazebag comments.

I cleared my throat. "She's a mutual friend and she's really cool. She decorated the beach house and we went skinny-dipping and then...I kissed her. And she's a damn good kisser. We're just friends, but we come with benefits."

"So, you aren't dating her?"

"No. I asked her to fool around so I could...forget about Alexia." I didn't like admitting the fact I was still wrapped around her finger. And I certainly didn't like admitting she was still in my thoughts. I wished she would leave, especially my dreams.

"What does she get out of this?"

"Other than good sex, I escort her for free. Her parents are assholes about her being single so I'm there to save the day."

He nodded. "Interesting arrangement. At least you finally made the plunge with a new woman."

"Well...we haven't actually done it yet."

He raised an eyebrow. "Yeah?"

"Just kissed. I'm really into her but...I just couldn't do it."

He rubbed his chin and faced forward.

I rubbed the back of my neck then studied the stage.

Kyle turned back to me after a few moments of silence. "You know what I think?"

"Not really."

He chuckled. "I'm going to tell you anyway, asshole."

"Great..."

"I think you can't have sex with someone unless you're in love with them."

Confusion hit me in a large wave. "How do you figure?"

"Before Alexia, you fucked anything that moved. But when you finally had her, you were happy for years. Even when you broke up, you still missed her. I think you're a lot more mature now and you can't go back to what you were. You won't admit it to yourself but I think you want another serious relationship."

"I don't," I said firmly.

"I know Alexia hurt you, and I'm not saying it wouldn't scar anybody. But keep in mind those three years before that you two were really happy. Everyone thought she was the woman you would marry."

I hated thinking about it. Somehow, the good memories were more painful than the ones.

"I think you want that again but with the right person. Therefore, you can't have meaningless sex with Harper."

"I don't want another relationship," I said firmly. "And I never want one again."

He sighed, knowing we were having the same argument we had a million times before. "I think if you gave it a chance you would feel differently."

"No."

"Fine," he said, growing aggravated. "Then sleep with this girl tonight."

"Maybe I will," I said with a growl.

"You won't." He shook his head. "I know you won't. You don't miss Alexia. You just miss what you had. And you're afraid that you'll never find that happiness again. That's what you're hurting over, not the actual person."

"Stop analyzing me, alright?" I hissed. "I'm not a patient."

"I'm just trying to help," he said calmly.

"Well, don't." I knew I was being vicious to my brother but I couldn't help it.

He looked at his watch and checked the time. "Show is about to start."

I ignored his attempt at normal conversation. Instead, I looked at anything but him.

***

When the show ended and the actors started to file onto the floor, Kyle and I moved to Nate. He was speaking to his fellow dancers, and when he saw me, his eyes lit up.

"You came!" He moved into my arms and hugged me hard.

"Of course," I said as I hugged him back. "And you did a great job."

"Thanks." He pulled away, gratitude still in his eyes. Then he shifted his gaze to my brother. It was clear he knew who he was. We looked so similar there was no room for mistake. "You must be Troy's brother. Nice to meet you." He shook his hand.

Kyle smiled and returned the embrace. "I'm slightly better-looking, obviously."

Nate chuckled then dropped his hand. He seemed a little flustered, almost nervous. His cheeks had a tint to them and he seemed different, not himself. "Yeah..."

"You guys are performing all week?" I asked, trying to dispel the sudden awkwardness.

"Yeah," Nate answered. "I won't have much of a life for the next two weeks."

"At least you're doing what you love," I said.

"Yeah." He looked around the auditorium. "I just wish my parents would come..." Sadness fell heavily on his shoulders.

I didn't have the heart to tell him about my last encounter with his mom and dad. All it would do is make him feel hopeless. And hopeless was exactly how I felt too. Nothing I said or did would change their mind. Even losing their son didn't make a difference. It was terrible.

Kyle's phone rang and he pulled it out of his pocket. "Excuse me for one moment." He stepped away and held the phone to his ear.

Nate watched him walk away. "Please tell me he's single." His voice came out high-pitched and excited.

"Uh...he has a boyfriend," I said. "They're living together, actually."

"Dammit." He kicked the floor. "He's so hot."

"Why, thank you," I said since my brother and I looked so much alike.

"You're welcome," he said with a laugh. "The good ones are always taken, I swear."

I immediately thought of Harper. How she was single was beyond my understanding. She could find Mr. Right easily because every guy would do what she wanted to be Mr. Right.

"Well, I should get back," Nate said. "Thank you for coming."

"Of course."

"And tell Kyle I said bye," he said. "And...let me know if it doesn't work out with his boyfriend."

I chuckled. "Will do."

Nate quickly hugged me. "I really appreciate your support. You have no idea what it means to me." He suddenly got emotional, his eyes coating with tears.

"You're my friend," I said. "And that's what friends do."

***

I had a new client, a girl name Patricia. From our coffee meeting I gathered that her boyfriend dumped her but he was still a mutual friend. Every time they went out, he was there. She wanted to make him jealous or prove that she was over him, and she wanted to prove that to all her friends too.

That's where I came in.

She was nice enough, and there wasn't anything about her that particularly annoyed me, but I wasn't looking forward to escorting her. I noticed that whenever I wasn't with Harper, that's where I wanted to be. She was usually on my mind, in some physical and lustful way. And I missed her friendship too. She was the coolest person I knew

I arrived at Patricia's door wearing jeans and a t-shirt. I wore an expensive watch to show her friends I had money since I couldn't wear a suit or anything. They were going out to a bar tonight so I had to wear casual attire.

She opened the door wearing a dress that was so short her ass practically hung out. She could wear whatever she wanted to wear, but I preferred women with a little more class. It was sexier to me. I'd rather imagine what I wasn't seeing instead of getting a face full of it. "Hey." She gave me a smile before she locked the door.

"Hey, Patricia," I said. "You look wonderful this evening." I had to put on my professional face and be the charming guy she paid me for. In real life, I was nothing even similar to charming. I was a jackass most of the time.

"Thanks." A slight tint came into her cheeks. "You do too."

I extended my arm and put it around her waist. "Shall we?"

"Sure." She walked beside me, having a difficult time in her heels.

I hated it when girls wore heels but couldn't walk in them. Then why wear them at all? Harper wore heels often but she walked like she was wearing sandals. It was natural to her. "How was your day?" Small talk was the worst but I had to do it.

"Good," she said. "Work was hectic." Then she launched into a fifteen-minute account of some girl in the finance department being a bitch because she didn't refill the paper tray for the printer. I nodded along and pretended to be interested. What was Harper doing? Maybe I could see her if the date ended early enough.

We reached the outside of the bar and she stilled in apprehension.

"You'll be fine," I said as I encouraged her. "You got me, remember?" I'd done this so many times that I knew how to read the signs. They felt pathetic that they had to hire a date, and it shook their confidence.

"Okay," she said as she released a deep breath.

I opened the door for her and we walked inside. My hand immediately moved to her waist and I pretended that she was the only woman who existed.

"Over there." She pulled me along with her, being affectionate with me.

We reached a table in the back, a large booth near the window. The lights were low and people were difficult to distinguish. Music was on in the background but I could still make out conversation. When we reached the table, I froze on the spot. A familiar brunette was sitting there, her hair curled and her blue eyes shining like gems. I would never forget that face as long as I lived.

Alexia.

Why the fuck was this happening to me?

I pulled myself together and pretended I hadn't noticed her. And if I had noticed her, I didn't care. I did a good job pretending she meant nothing to me at the grocery store.

"Hey, everyone," Patricia said with a perky voice.

"What have you brought with you?" a blonde friend said, eye-fucking the shit out of me.

"This is my boyfriend, Troy." Her attitude picked up when she saw the look of approval in everyone's eyes.

Alexia knew I was an escort so she probably knew what was going on. Would she be a bitch and rat her friend out? Or would she let it go? I really had no idea what she would do. It didn't make a difference to me. But I did wish I was nowhere near her. The nightmares finally stopped and now they would come back after looking at her face.

Patricia and I scooted into the booth, but once I was there, I wanted to leave. "Can I get you a drink, baby?" I turned to Patricia and gave her a fake look of affection.

"Cosmo, please."

I stood up. "Can I get anything for you, ladies?" I asked politely.

"No, thank you." The blonde batted her eyelashes at me.

"I can get my own. "Alexia slid out of the booth and stood up.

Now we were way too close together. Just being near her pissed me off. I wanted to run away, but I wanted to yell at her at the same time. I never had the opportunity to tell her how much she hurt me. I never got to scream.

Unsure what to say, I turned and walked away. I headed for the bar, grateful I could turn my back and drop my look of indifference. I was going to order a beer but now I might have to get a scotch. How would I survive this night? I had to control my hatred around Alexia but I had to pretend to be in love with Patricia at the same time. How would I ever pull this off? "Scotch," I said to the bartender. "Make it a double. And a cosmo." I hated it when girls drank fruity drinks. Harper drank gin—because she was hot.

"Your plan seems to be working." Her dreamy voice reached me and scratched my ears like nails on a chalkboard.

I didn't turn to Alexia. I stared straight ahead, making sure she didn't feel important or special. "I just hope you aren't a bitch and blow it."

"Patricia is my friend. I would never do that."

What the hell was taking the bartender so long?

"You seem flustered." She came closer to me, her arm touching mine.

I recoiled like a snake. "Don't touch me." My words came out venomous.

She did as I asked but didn't walk away. "This is going to be a long night if we can't get along..."

"Why do we have to talk at all?" I snapped. "Just go away."

She remained rooted to the spot. "You still hate me." Resignation was in her voice.

I wanted to grab a chair and break it on the bar. Anger coursed through me in waves. My skull was about to split from the scorching heat burning from my brain. I wanted to strangle this woman and watch her die in my arms. "What the hell do you think?" I finally turned to her, seeing that comely face I wish had no effect on me. "You think we're just going to be friends? What the fuck is wrong with you?"

Her eyes were guarded and it was impossible to tell what she was thinking, like always. Even in our relationship, her inner thoughts were a mystery to me. Perhaps if I'd known, I would have predicted the epic way she ripped out my heart. "Troy, it's been over a year. I just thought you would have let it go by now."

"Let it go?" I released a laugh even though the situation was anything but funny. "We were together for three years and then you just left me. And you lied about it. I had to see you with some guy to figure out what really happened. And I was going to propose...I had the ring and everything." Why did I tell her that? I was showing her my weakness and I hated myself for it. I was so fucking pathetic.

Her eyes softened for the first time in years. She regarded me differently, like she saw me as a new person. "You were going to propose...?"

"Why do you think I wanted to go to the Grand Canyon?" I spat. "Just because? I told you that place is just a dump and there's nothing to see."

Her eyes softened further. "That's where you were going to do it?"

Why was I still talking to her? Why was I standing here? I was being paid to be someone else's date, not stand here and go to battle with my ex. I hated the fact I was still attached to her, in some odd way. I hated the fact that when I looked at her, I still thought she was beautiful. "Fuck off, Alexia." I grabbed the drinks the second the bartender put them down and hightailed it to my table.

Patricia grabbed the drink and took a sip. "What took so long?"

"I was talking to your friend Alexia. She's very nice." I put on a fake face and pretended my heart wasn't broken all over again. Why did I have to tell Alexia I was about to propose? Why couldn't I just let go of the past and move on?

Alexia returned to the table with her drink and sat right across from me.

I looked at anything but her, pretending she was a stranger. I kept my focus on Patricia, acting as a loving boyfriend that only cared about her. Her dress rose up when she sat down because it was already so short. But I didn't look. I thought about the one thing that gave me comfort.

Harper.

***

The second I dropped off Patricia at her door, I called Harper. It was late but I wanted to see her.

"Muh?" she said on the fifth ring. She was clearly asleep.

"Did I wake you, sleepyhead?" I teased. The second I heard her voice I was in a better mood.

"Ugh...hmm."

I cocked an eyebrow. "I don't understand gibberish, Harper."

"What do you want?" she finally said in a raspy voice.

"To see you, of course."

"It's almost one in the morning," she argued.

"But I miss you." I meant it. I meant it more than I realized.

"I'm too tired, Troy..."

"Can I sleep with you?" The last person I slept with was Alexia. The idea of sleeping so close to someone didn't sound appetizing at all. But with Harper, it did.

"I'm not in the mood to get busy tonight."

I laughed because she sounded half-dead. "I meant just sleep with you." I didn't want to be alone right now. I was too depressed. My conversation with Alexia was making me feel worse with every passing second.

"Okay," she said. "But I look like hell right now."

"I highly doubt that."

"Let me paint a picture for you," she said. "Messy bun, plaid pajama bottoms, and a t-shirt stained with syrup."

"Why syrup?" I asked.

"Because I love waffles, alright? Get off my case."

"You could wash your shirt..." She was such an odd ball sometimes.

"Or I could just go to bed and not care."

I kept walking then entered her apartment building. "I'm almost there. I suggest you change your shirt."

"Nope. You're dropping by, and I refuse to accommodate someone stopping by at one in the morning."

"Then I'll lick the syrup away."

"You would," she said.

I reached her door and knocked. "Your Prince Charming has arrived."

"Wait until you see your Cinderella." She hung up then opened the door. She wore baggy pajama bottoms and a gray t-shirt with an obvious brown stain right in the front. Her hair was a mess and her face was free of make up. "Damn, you look hot," I said sarcastically.

She smacked my arm. "Shut up!"

I laughed. "Guys must be drooling all over you."

"You know what? If you're going to make fun of me then forget it." She tried to shut the door.

I burst inside before she could keep me out. "I'm kidding."

"Liar."

My arms moved around her waist and I pulled her close to me. She stopped fighting me immediately and actually melted at my touch. I could feel it and see it. Then I gave her a warm kiss. It made me feel alive. When I pulled away, I rubbed my nose against hers. "You want the truth?"

"Always."

"I think you look adorable." I eyed the stain on the front of her shirt. "Even if you're really messy."

A genuine smile broke out on her lips. "Yeah?"

"Oh yeah." My hand moved under her shirt and up her naked back. She wasn't wearing a bra and I loved the feel of her soft skin. The petite muscles of her back excited me. I couldn't explain why. "Can I join you in bed?"

"It's a miracle I'm awake now."

"When did you become an old woman?" I teased.

"When I got a big girl job and started having responsibilities."

I rolled my eyes. "Why can't you have both?"

She shrugged. "Too tired."

"Well, let's head to bed." I scooped her up and carried her in my arms.

"My Prince Charming is carrying me over the threshold," she said in a snooty voice.

E. L. Todd

I entered her bedroom and placed her on the bed with the rumpled sheets. "Do you dance in your sleep?" I asked when I examined the bed.

"I toss and turn sometimes..." She got under the covers and sighed.

I stripped off my clothes down to my boxers then I lay beside her. She had a queen bed, which was a downgrade for me. I slept in a California King because of my height and size.

She turned on her side and faced me. "So?"

"So?" I snuggled with her and pulled her close to me. Her leg was hooked over my waist and our chests were pressed together. Her hand moved up my stomach and rested on the skin over my heart.

"Why are you here at one in the morning unless you wanted to get laid?"

"I missed you."

"And that's it?" she asked incredulously.

I shrugged.

"What happened to honesty, Troy?" She gave me that firm look I'd grown accustomed to.

The sadness enveloped me like a fog and I suddenly couldn't find any reason to be happy. And the fact I felt this way and was unable to fight it off made me feel worse. "I saw Alexia."

Her stern expression softened and she looked at me with pity. Her hand moved up my chest to my shoulder. She rubbed the muscle gently before she dug her fingers into my hair and played with the strands. "I'm sorry, Troy."

"Yeah..." I swallowed the lump in my throat and moved my hand up her waist until I reached the area of her ribcage. She was so small. My hand could take up her entire stomach. I could crush her if I really wanted to.

She stared at me, silently asking me to open up to her.

"I was with a client, and that client happened to be friends with her. I tried to ignore Alexia, but she cornered me at the bar and said she wished I didn't hate her, that a year was long enough to get over what happened. But then I said something really stupid."

"What?" she asked.

"I told her I was going to propose right before she dumped me. The look of pity she gave me..." I shook my head. "I wish I hadn't said that. I wish I could have a do-over."

"What's done is done," she said gently. "And I hope it made her feel terrible."

I shook my head slightly. "I wish I didn't care about making her feel terrible. I want to walk into a room with her and not even care that she's there. That's all I want. I don't ask for much."

Harper continued to stroke my hair gently, with a loving touch. Her face was just inches from mine.

"My brother told me I don't miss her at all. Actually, I just miss that relationship we have. I want to have that again but with the right person. I'm just too scared. That's the real reason I have issues. And I resent her for that."

"I agree with him."

"You do?" I asked.

"You just need to let it go and give someone else a chance."

I stared at her beautiful face, noting the flawless skin and gorgeous eyes. She just woke up but she was still magnificent. "I wish I could give you a chance." I didn't think when I spoke. I just said what was on my mind. Harper had become one of my closest friends. To say I adored her was an understatement.

"Maybe one day you will," she whispered.

I released a sarcastic laugh. "You're way out of my league, Harper. Let's be honest here."

"Where do you get that from?"

"First of all, you're gorgeous. Second of all, you're super cool. And third of all, I'm some loser who may or may not be hung up on my ex. The guy you end up with should spot you on the street and immediately know you are his future wife. You deserve a fairytale love story, not a man who uses you to get over someone else."

She massaged my scalp. "I think you're being too hard on yourself. The only quality I despise is deceit. As long as you're honest with me, I don't think less of you. If you were sleeping with me just to get over your ex without telling me, then I would hate you. But that's not that you did, Troy."

I shook my head. "Still not good enough for you, Harper. End of story."

She cupped my face and kissed the corner of my mouth. "I think you're one of the most wonderful men I've ever met."

"Yeah?" I whispered.

"I do. You're my friend and I love you."

My heart kicked into overdrive and I felt winded. Those last words made me spiral out of control then land with a loud thud. I knew what context she meant them in but it still gave me chills. "I love you too, Harper."

She smiled at me. "Now stop saying mean things about my friend."

I smiled. "Sorry."

"Because if you mess with him, you mess with me."

"Got it."

Her hand returned to my chest and she closed her eyes, getting ready to sleep.

I was tired and relaxed but I didn't want to sleep. All I wanted to do was stare at her.

And that's what I did.

***

Rhett texted me a few days later. *You can't avoid me forever, man.*

He and I hadn't spoken since I walked out on him. He pinned me down and knew exactly who I was. He knew I was lying about my promiscuous lifestyle, and he knew I was lying about Alexia. The fact he figured me out so easily bothered me the most. I was embarrassed I didn't do a better job convincing him otherwise. I ignored his message then tuned my guitar.

If you don't respond, I'm just going to stop by your apartment. I've given you enough space.

Fucking asshole. I assumed this problem would just go away by itself. Apparently, Rhett wouldn't let it go. He let me slide by with my lies but now he had enough. The bad thing about having a best friend is having someone who knew you better than you knew yourself. It was fucking annoying.

So, what's it going to be?

I was cornered. I'd rather meet him somewhere instead of having him stop by at a random time. It was the lesser of two evils. *Fine. Beer?*

Good choice. I'll see you in an hour.
***

Rhett was already there when I walked inside. I grabbed a beer then slid into the booth across from him. The bar was quiet and there weren't many people around. The silence bothered me. I wish it were loud so it would drown out my thoughts.

Rhett's beer sat in front of him, and judging the foam on top, he hadn't touched it.

I stared at him then looked out the window, saying nothing.

He didn't say anything either.

Silence stretched forever.

"So...?" I turned back to him. "What's up?"

"I'm waiting for you to tell me that." He rested his hand on the glass but didn't take a drink.

I hated it when people put me on the spot, waiting for me to talk first. It gave them all the power.

"So, Harper is decorating your beach house?"

The topic of Harper was safe. "Yeah, she did a great job. It looks brand new."

He nodded. "You like her?"

This quickly went south. " She's my friend. Of course, I like her."

"And she's only your friend?" he asked.

I hated lying to Rhett. It was one thing to hide something from him but another thing to totally lie. "I think she's really hot. But yeah, she's just a friend."

He seemed to believe me. "She's really cute and pretty cool. I think you guys would get along well if you gave it a chance."

"You're encouraging me to date her?" I asked incredulously.

"You aren't a dick like you pretend to be, and I knew you wouldn't be a dick to her."

I drank my beer just to have something to do.

"So...let's talk about Alexia now. You've put it off long enough."

I sighed in irritation. "I don't want to talk about it."

"That's too damn bad," he snapped. "I'm your best friend. Talk to me, man."

"There's nothing to say."

"When have I ever given you the impression I judge you? For anything?" Hurt was in his voice. It seemed like it truly bothered him that I kept my thoughts to myself.

"Why does it bother you so much?" I asked.

"Because I always thought we told each other everything. Apparently, I was completely wrong. As soon as Alexia left, you became a different person. I thought giving you space was the right thing to do at the time, but now I realize my mistake. If I'd opened you up then, you might not be so closed off now."

"Don't do that, man," I said quietly. "Don't blame yourself."

"Well, it's too late. Now talk to me."

I didn't realize how much my silence was hurting my best friend. "Okay, fine."

He drank his beer for the first time and waited for me to speak.

"She left me for someone else."

Rhett didn't react in any noticeable way. His eyes didn't even flinch, like he already suspected what I said.

"She lied and made up some bullshit excuse about her being the problem...I wasn't sure why I believed her. Then I saw her with some other guy...I felt like an idiot. I still feel like an idiot. I had the ring and I was going to take her to the Grand Canyon to propose. But she dumped me a few days before."

Rhett looked down at his beer for a moment. When he looked up at me, sympathy was in his eyes. "That would break anyone, Troy. There's no reason to be ashamed of that."

"I just feel stupid for not seeing it coming." I stared at a spot on the table and concentrated on that. "She was obviously cheating on me when we were together and I didn't even notice. I was just too happy and too in love to notice what was right in front of me."

"And you don't want to fall in love again because you couldn't go through that again."

I nodded in response.

"I don't blame you for feeling like this, Troy. It's completely understandable."

"Yeah?" I asked. "Because it seems like everyone is trying to change me and force me to get over it."

"I think you do need to get over it," he said bluntly. "But I also understand why it's hard for you. I don't think less of you for that."

"I would if I could, Rhett. It's just not possible."

"It is possible," he said gently. "Just because one woman hurt you like that doesn't mean another one will. Don't throw away your future because of your past."

"I just can't..." I closed my eyes.

"Take it slow. Go on a few dates."

"No."

Rhett sighed and backed off. "I'm happy for you and Aspen. She's a great girl. But not everyone can have that, Rhett."

"No," he agreed. "But I know you can."

I shook my head and looked away.

"Maybe you just need more time. Three years is a long time to be with the same person. One day, you will be over it. One day, you'll be able to trust someone again."

"I highly doubt that. And I really don't want to be that boyfriend that goes through a girl's phone and checks up on her. I'll never trust her and that's not fair to her."

"That's why I think you should date first. Just have fun and meet new girls. Most women want a good-looking faithful guy to settle down with. And they have no intention of cheating. Alexia was just a bitch. Don't compare other women to her."

"I know you're right," I said. "I know it. But that doesn't change the way I feel. I've lost all faith in relationships. I really don't think I can get it back."

"You can," he said firmly. "You can have what I have with Aspen."

"Not now, " I said. "And probably not ever."

Harper

I was freaking out.

I'd never introduced a guy to my parents before, and now I was bringing Troy, who wasn't even my real boyfriend. So many things could go wrong, and if they caught me in my lie, it would be worse than me admitting I was single.

Please go smoothly tonight.

Troy knocked on the door and made me jump two feet into the air.

Shit, I needed to calm down.

I opened the door and saw him stand on the other side in a full suit and tie.

"What?" he asked with a blank expression. "You look like you just saw a ghost."

"Why are you wearing a suit?" I demanded.

"Uh...thanks. You look great too."

I rubbed my temple. "It's just dinner at my parents. You're dressed too formal and we're already running late and you don't have time to change..."

"Okay, I'm not used to uptight Harper." He came inside and shut the door. Then he took off his jacket and removed his tie. "There. Now I'm pretty casual. You can calm down now."

"Sorry...I know I'm freaking out over nothing."

"And that's my best suit. I look awesome in it."

"You looked very sexy, Troy." I walked into the bathroom and finished my make up.

"Very sexy?" he asked. "That's all I'm getting?"

"You looked totally fuckable," I shouted from the bathroom. "Is that better?"

"A little..."

I adjusted my cardigan then messed with my hair again. I was never comfortable in my own skin around my family. My mom always said I needed to be thinner like my sister, and my hair looked like a bird's nest. Nothing I did was good enough.

Troy came to the doorway then leaned against the panel. He stared at me with his arms across his chest.

"What?" I asked, still looking in the mirror.

"You look beautiful," he said seriously.

I rolled my eyes. "Not now, Troy."

"Hey." He grabbed my wrist and pulled me to him. "I mean it."

"You would still say that even if you didn't."

"No, I'm a hundred percent honest with you—always."

I knew I was being a brat right now. The stress was getting to me.

"Now will you calm the fuck down?" he demanded.

"I can try." I moved from his embrace then checked my appearance in the mirror one more time. I wore black pants and pearls. My hair was big and slightly curled. I looked like I came from money, not that it was a good quality. "Let's get this over with."

He put his arm around my waist. "We're going to have fun tonight."

"Wait until you meet my parents," I warned.

"I'm sure they aren't as bad as you think."

"Fine," I snapped. "Prove me wrong."

"I will," he said firmly.

I grabbed my purse then we walked down to the street to his Maserati. He opened the passenger door for me to get inside, which surprised me and I didn't know why, and then got behind the driver's seat.

"They live in Connecticut, right?"

"Yeah," I answered.

He migrated through traffic until we were on the open road. "So, I'll be rich and sophisticated. I'm sure your parents will like that."

"No," I said immediately. "Just be yourself, Troy."

"Be myself?" he asked incredulously. "You can barely stand me when I'm myself."

"Troy, you're great. Let that come out."

"I don't think that's what parents want to hear."

"Well, if you're snooty and annoying, everyone is going to have a hard time believing I'm really dating you. My personality would never sync up with someone like that. So, be yourself."

"How about I be myself, for the most part, but cut out a few things."

"That's reasonable."

"Okay." He grabbed my hand and held it on my thigh. His touch was unexpected, and it didn't seem like he even noticed how odd it was. He didn't seem to think twice about it because he didn't look at me. We'd never held hands before, but I liked the warmth. My fingers linked with his, and I stared at the different sizes of our hands. His was big enough to cover my entire face. Mine was small enough to barely wrap around his shaft.

Then he brought my hand to his lips and kissed the knuckles. "Everything will be fine. I'll get you through this."

My spine shivered at the sweet gesture. "Okay."

***

Troy pulled up to the roundabout then parked the car. "Sweet place," he said as he whistled.

My parents had a large house and a few acres of land. It was most people's dream home, but my parents complained that they didn't have a house closer to the coast. That's how annoying they were. "Yeah."

"This place must have been a babe magnet when you were growing up."

"Yeah...I was bringing back girls all the time."

He nudged my side playfully. "You know what I mean. You didn't sneak boys into your room for a romp romp?"

I cocked an eyebrow. "I've never heard anyone call it that in my life."

"You need to get with the times, Perfect Ten."

"Whatever, Eight Inches."

He smiled before he got out of the car and opened my door for me. He grabbed my hand and helped me out. Then he held me close and gave me a gentle and quick kiss. His face was close to mine and he rubbed our noses together.

His embraces caught me off guard every time. He was such a good kisser, and every touch was sensual and amazing. He made me feel loved without even trying.

"I'm sure your parents are watching us through the window," he explained.

"Oh." *I thought that was just for me.*

"Not that I didn't enjoy it." He grabbed my hand and walked with me to the front door.

Troy looked delicious in his buttoned up shirt and slacks. His muscles were clear in his stance, and he held himself like a soldier. His ass looked great, but his best feature was his face. He was attractive in a classic way, but he had a few boyish charms to make him adorable at the same time. There wasn't a single thing I'd change about him.

We reached the front door and Troy knocked. "Showtime." He was cool and suave, in his own element and in control. He did this for a living. Meanwhile, I was practically panicked and terrified. Troy watched me and spotted my unease. "Where's my girl?"

I turned to him, unsure of his meaning.

"The woman I know is fierce and strong. She doesn't take shit from anybody and she's not scared of anything. Who cares what they think? I already know you're amazing and I actually know you. Their opinion is irrelevant."

The fact Troy, of all people, could knock some sense into me told me I needed to get my head on straight and stop acting like a coward. "You're right..."

"I'm always right."

My head snapped in his direction. "I wouldn't say that."

"I would." He gave me that smile I'd fallen more in love with every time he gave it.

I was about to give a smart-ass comment when the door flew open.

Troy quickly hugged me into his side and gave a charming smile.

I turned to my parents, remembering the chore I had to do.

Mom's eyes widened when she looked at Troy. Judging the stunned look on her face, she didn't think it was possible that me, the older, less attractive sister, could land a guy as good-looking as him. It hurt, but it also made me feel vengeful, like I was proving her wrong.

"Hello, Mr. Peterson." Troy took the lead and shook Dad's hand. "Thank you for having us for dinner."

Dad shook it, and nodded in excitement.

Then Troy turned to Mom and shook her hand. "I see where Harper gets her beauty from. It's a pleasure to meet you, Mrs. Peterson."

My jaw was about to drop. I didn't think it was possible for Troy to be so slick.

"You're so charming," Mom said as she chuckled and brushed his comment away. "The pleasure is all mine."

Like I didn't exist, they ignored me.

"Please come in, Troy." Mom ushered him inside and put her hand on his back.

They weren't even going to say hi to me?

Troy stopped and turned to me. The look in his eyes told me exactly what he was thinking, that he understood I was hurt that he was the only thing that mattered to my parents. "Wait, can't forget my lovely date." He came to me and took me by the hand. "I hardly go anywhere without my other half." He looked down into my face with nothing but affection. *Was it genuine? Or was he just doing his job?*

"Awe..." Mom leaned toward Dad. "So cute together..."

Still haven't said hi to me, but whatever.

We came into the living room, where Kara and Sebastian were sitting. A bit of jealousy rushed into my body. Kara was always the beautiful, more attractive sister. Troy would probably think the same thing and wish she were the sister he was messing around with.

"You must be Kara." Troy approached her and shook her hand. "Congratulations on the engagement and the baby."

"Oh...thank you." She looked stunned by his appearance. Then she stood up and shook his hand awkwardly, like she too couldn't believe I brought home a model to meet the family.

When Troy shook hands with Sebastian, Kara looked at me. "Holy shit, he's hot," she mouthed to me.

"I know," I mouthed back.

"Where did you find him?" she mouthed again.

"Let's talk about this later."

Troy and Sebastian exchanged introductions before Troy came back to my side and put his arm around my waist. "You have a beautiful family, Harper."

"Thanks..." I leaned toward his ear. "What happened to being yourself?"

Mom and Dad came into the room.

"Dinner is almost ready." Mom waddled into the kitchen and prepared the feast. "Just a few more minutes."

"Can't wait," Troy said politely. "I love a home-cooked meal."

"Can I get you anything?" Dad asked. "Wine?"

"Sure," Troy said. "Thank you. I'll take wine."

I glared at my dad. "I'll take one too. And hi, by the way."

Dad gave me a fake smile then walked away.

Ugh, I hated my family.

Troy stuck to my side like glue. "It's not that bad," he whispered.

"I wish we were at your beach house," I blurted.

"So we can skinny dip?" he asked with a smug look.

"So I can lay in the sun and forget my troubles."

"While on my lap, right?" he asked.

I rolled my eyes at him.

Sebastian came up to Troy. "So, you own an online dating company?"

"Yeah," Troy answered. "It started off as a small project then quickly expanded. It was the best decision I ever made—except finding the girl of my dreams." He gave me a pointed look.

"Awe," Kara whispered and fanned her face.

"Sports fan?" Sebastian asked.

"Definitely," Troy said. "I watch everything, even golf."

Sebastian smiled. "We'll get along just fine." Then they became deep in a conversation about the NFL draft and I was ignored again.

Kara pulled me a few feet away. "Harper!"

What? "Kara!"

"Troy is gorgeous. Why have you been hiding him?"

Because I don't want to share him with anyone. "We were taking it slow..."

"Well, speed it up," she said. "I thought Sebastian was the most handsome man in the world but…"

I glared at her. "But what?"

Kara seemed to know she crossed the line. "I'm just saying you did good. And he's so sweet."

"You hardly know him," I countered.

"Well, my fiancé clearly loves him. Look at them going at it."

We both watched Troy and Sebastian carry on their heated debate about the new quarterback drafted for the Forty-Niners.

"Well, guys always get along when they talk about sports," I said.

"And girls never get along even when they are talking about hair," she said. "Is he the one, Harper?"

"Uh…"

"He's so in love with you. He better be the one." She crossed her arms over her chest and gave me a firm look. She wasn't backing down.

"Again, you don't know him very well."

"I know everything I need to know."

"You mean, the fact he's rich, is good-looking, and likes sports."

"Are you telling me he's not a good guy?" she asked with a raised eyebrow. "Because you're spending more time convincing me I shouldn't like him rather than actually like him."

I blew up. "I'm just irritated that the only time my family is interested in me is when a guy is involved. I'm perfectly capable of being on my own."

Her eyes softened and she dropped her defensive stance. "We just want you to be happy. Sebastian makes me happier than I've ever been. We all just want the same for you. You're missing out."

"Boyfriend or no boyfriend, I'm very happy."

"I'm not saying you need a man," she said. "But having one—especially one as fine as that—is never a bad thing."

Just when I opened my mouth to argue, Mom announced dinner. "Take your seats, everyone."

Troy found me like he had me on radar. He pulled me into his side. "Thought I lost you for a moment there." He pulled me into his body and I could feel the hardness of his body against mine.

Kara watched our interaction closely.

"You could never lose me."

He grinned when he looked down at me and then he placed a gentle kiss on my forehead.

"Awe," Kara whispered.

I ignored her and enjoyed the touch, no matter how fake it was.

"Let's get our seats." Troy pulled me away and escorted me to the dining room. He pulled out my chair for me before he took the seat beside me. Then his hand moved to my thigh, naturally.

Dad took the seat beside him. "Was that a Maserati I saw outside?"

"Indeed," Troy answered. "She's my girl."

"She's a beauty," Dad agreed. "How old is she?"

"Just a year," Troy answered. "Before that I had a Range Rover. I definitely like the feel of the car more."

Dad nodded.

I stared blankly at my glass of wine, wondering when this stupid dinner would be over.

Everyone was fascinated by Troy. They asked him every question you could think of, and they all looked at him with approval. He was the knight in shining armor of the evening. Even when they asked questions about our relationship, they were directed at Troy, not me. It made no sense at all. They were so concerned about me settling down with someone, but they didn't care at all about me as a person. It baffled me.

Quiet conversation continued around the table as we ate quietly. Mom had honeyed ham and mashed potatoes with a side of greens. Her cooking was good and I missed it sometimes but I never missed her company.

Troy was pretty much being interrogated. They asked him where he grew up, where he went to college, and if he ever considered modeling.

"Mom." I gave her a look that told her to back off.

"What?" she asked innocently.

Troy laughed it off. "I've actually done a few ads in the past—nothing fancy."

"I'm a model too," Kara said.

"Cool," he said. "We probably have a lot in common then."

Sebastian put a protective arm over her shoulders.

I tried not to roll my eyes.

When dinner was finished and dessert was served, neither one of my parents had spoken to me. Only Kara and Sebastian acknowledged my existence. I was getting fed up with it. I didn't ask for much, just a little attention, and positive attention. Not, "When are you going to go back to school and find a more promising career? When are you going to bring a man home?" All I wanted was for someone to ask me how my day was going. That's it. But nope, I never got it.

Pissed off, I stood up and excused myself wordlessly. No one probably even noticed, except Troy. I grabbed my purse then walked out the front door and sat on the steps. The cool evening air chilled my angry temperature slightly, but the fumes of my rage still burned. I opened my purse and pulled out a cigarette and lit it. I hardly ever smoked, only when I was really upset. I took a few drags and enjoyed the soothing affect. Then I purposely put it out on one of the vases outside. They probably cared more about that plant than they cared about me.

The front door opened behind me then quickly closed. Heavy footsteps came down before someone sat beside me on the steps.

I didn't turn and look and I didn't need to. I knew who it was.

"You missed the mousse cake," Troy said. "It was delicious."

"I'll have to take your word for it."

His knee touched mine and he rested his hands on his thighs. "They're really nice people."

"They are?" I asked curiously. "I wouldn't know."

He grabbed my hand and squeezed it. His eyes were fixed on me but I refused to look his way. "Why would your parents care that much about you settling down if they didn't care about you?" His voice came out quiet.

"Their reputation."

"To who?" he asked. "It's not like they're celebrities."

"No, but they still like to brag about Kara to their friends. When people ask about me, Mom and Dad obviously don't know what to say. I'm just a failure to them."

"They don't think that," he said calmly. "I admit they aren't the warmest people, but just because they struggle to show they care doesn't mean they don't. You can't read their mind."

"I don't even feel welcome here. The sad part is, this is the most welcome I've felt in a long time—because I had a man to bring along."

He squeezed my hand again. Then he leaned his face close to me. "Don't let it get you down. They wouldn't be so interested in me if I weren't dating you."

"I know you probably think my behavior is stupid and I get that, but you just don't understand."

"I think I do, actually," he said quietly. "My brother has been gay his whole life and my parents won't accept him. To them, he's just an embarrassment. To them, he's the kid that failed. At least your parents accept who you love and encourage it."

"Don't compare us," I said. "The situations are completely different."

"They are," he admitted. "But my point is, maybe they aren't extremely warm toward you but they never want to lose you just because you do something they don't approve of. If you told them you were a lesbian, they wouldn't be happy but they wouldn't disown you either."

I pulled my hand from his and crossed my arms over my chest.

"Knock it off," he snapped.

My head turned in his direction.

"You can close off from everyone else but you can't close off from me." He lifted me and shifted me to his lap. I automatically wrapped my arms around his neck and held on. Our faces were close together, and I could feel him breathe. He looked into my face and examined me. "Never close off from me." His fingers moved to my cheek, and they trailed the skin until they reached my lips. He touched them lightly then lowered his hand.

Silence echoed around us, and for just a second, it felt like we were the only people on the planet. The stars and the moon were our only company. Troy looked at me in a new way, like he was seeing a side to me he never noticed before. The usual smug look in his eyes was gone, replaced by a calm curiosity. The emotion that shined in his eyes was different, unidentifiable. Then he placed a finger under my chin and slowly inched my lips toward his.

He kissed me in a way he never had before. His lips lightly caressed mine, like he was afraid they would break if he pushed me too hard. Every breath he took was audible on my ears because it was so quiet. Our lips moved together, making a light smacking noise. The sound loosened the muscles in my core and made me crave more.

Troy wrapped both arms tightly around me, forming walls of titanium, and deepened the kiss further. It became more intense but the softness was the same. We breathed into each other's mouths, taking as much as was aloud. One hand snaked into my hair and he gripped it tightly like I was under his control. I loved the way he touched me, like I was his and no one else's.

Troy moved his lips to my neck and gave me the touch I craved. He somehow knew I loved it because he continued to do it. He was the only guy who understood what I liked and disliked without me having to explain it to him.

Then he moved back to my lips and gave me one final, long embrace. He let the kiss linger for seconds before he finally pulled away. His eyes emitted their own light while he looked at me. There was an expression there I couldn't distinguish, like an image in an art galley that created a certain emotion, but what the image was itself was unknown.

He pulled me closer to his chest like he didn't want to let me go then buried his face in my neck. His hand gripped me tightly, like he thought I might fly away. "I'm sorry you're hurting. Believe me, it hurts me."

His words spiraled into my heart.

"I think you deserve better than this, and it's wrong that your family doesn't see all the beautiful things about you, like I do, but the situation could be worse. The only person who can determine your value is you, not me or your family. So don't let them bring you down."

"I know you're right," I whispered.

He kissed my forehead and left his lips there for a long time. "I'm always right."

A slight smile came to my lips. "I don't know about that..."

"I do," he said.

"At least my parents believe you're in love with me. That's quite a feat."

"It wasn't that hard." He looked into my eyes as he said it.

I stared back, unsure what to do or say.

"Want to get out of here?" he whispered. "I'll tell them you aren't feeling well."

"There's nothing I want more," I said immediately.

***

The drive was spent in silence, and when we walked into my apartment, it was clear Troy intended to stick around. I didn't want him to leave anyway. It was like having a super hot best friend all the time.

Once we walked into the bedroom, I knew something was different about tonight. I felt it. And I could tell he did too. He stared at me in the dark. The limited light coming through the window displaced his face and body. Slowly, he unbuttoned his shirt then tossed it on the floor.

His body was a slab of marble. A perfectionist chiseled every inch of him. The lines and grooves continued endlessly. One of my favorite features was his narrowed hips, which led into an obvious V. A light trail of hair disappeared into his slacks. Other than the hair on his arms, legs, and head, that was all he had.

He watched me like a hunter in the forest. Every move I made, no matter how slight, was obvious to him. He stepped toward me, a dark intent clear in his blue eyes. He stopped in front of me then looked down into my face. His height surpassed mine by a foot, but I liked the way he towered over me.

One hand moved to the front of my shirt and deliberately unbuttoned my cardigan until it was completely open, showing my deep purple bra. Without shame, he looked down at me, his eyes focused on the obvious line of cleavage my push up bra formed. Then he pushed it off my shoulders, the greed obvious in the way he ripped it off like it meant nothing. With one hand again, he unbuttoned my jeans and unzipped them. He fingered the top of my panties, feeling the soft lace. His fingers moved in further until they reached the nub between my legs. He pressed his face close to mine then touched me with the perfect amount of pressure.

I automatically gripped his arms and held on as he touched me. It felt so good because I hadn't been touched there in so long. But it also felt good because Troy knew exactly what he was doing. He made me wet, and soon my panties were soaked. My breathing increased even though I wished it wouldn't, and soon I was desperate for him, to feel more than just his fingers.

He stared at me but didn't kiss me, examining my face while he touched me. I thought it would make me self-conscious but it didn't. It only made the fire in my belly burn more. He slowly pulled his fingers away, making me wince, and then inserted them in his mouth. He sucked my juice off while looking into my eyes. Then he pulled my pants down to my ankles.

He kneeled down so I balanced myself by gripping his shoulders. When my pants were completely off he went for my thong. He slowly pulled it down my legs, like he was enjoying the slow way we moved. When they were free, he moved his mouth to the area between my legs and gave my nub a gentle kiss.

"Oh my god…" I immediately squeezed his shoulder because it felt amazing. His tongue circled my clitoris then penetrated deep inside me.

Troy moved on leg over his shoulder, forcing me to use him for balance. With my legs spread wider, he kissed me harder and with more pressure.

I was shaking because my nerves wouldn't stop firing off. He was sending too much pleasure in my body and it was making me pant like a dog. I gripped his hair and moaned loudly, unable to control myself anymore. Just when I was about to hit the edge he pulled away and stood up.

I wanted to scream because I missed his mouth so much. My hands went for his slacks and I practically ripped them off. He needed to get naked as quickly as possible. I wanted him inside me, now. I got them off then yanked his boxers away. The long shaft leaned outward, and he was every inch of the man he claimed. And he was thick to top it off.

I knew he wanted to see me on my knees, like every other guy, so I lowered myself then gripped his thighs as my mouth found his tip. The second my tongue touched the head of his dick, he released a moan from deep in his throat. One hand fisted my hair like he wanted to shove my mouth far onto his length.

I inserted him as far as I could go and then I used both hands to massage his shaft while I sucked his tip.

He breathed hard, and his eyes darkened. "Fuck, you give good head."

I kept going, giving him my best moves since he did the same to me. I practically unhinged my jaw trying to take in his length and width.

"I love that big mouth." He pulled my head back and pulled his cock out. Then he picked me up off the floor like I didn't weigh anything and laid me on the bed. He moved over me, covering my small size with his expansive one.

I was so eager for him. I'd never wanted sex this bad. I was willing to beg for it, plead, whatever he wanted.

His lips found mine, and he kissed me hard, devouring my mouth like he needed it to survive. My legs wrapped around his waist, and he felt one thigh with his hand, touching the smooth skin from my knee to my ass. His kissed moved down my neck and he unclasped my bra with one hand. Most guys couldn't even do it with two. He sucked each nipple until they were raw before he looked down at me. "Do you have condoms?"

"My nightstand." *Yes, this was happening.* I hadn't had a decent lay in months, and if Troy could do all those things with over-the-top perfection then I knew he could fuck like a sailor.

He snaked his hand inside and pulled one out. Using his teeth to rip the foil, he got it open then rolled it onto his length. It was a pink color and cherry scent. After he secured it around the base of his cock and checked the tip for space, he positioned himself over me.

Troy was the most handsome man I'd been with, and I'd thought about this moment dozens of time. He was cocky and full of himself most of the time, and he certainly didn't understand boundaries, but he was sweet and sensitive beneath all the bullshit he projected. I found the knowledge endearing and it made me care more about him. I hated Alexia for what she'd done to him, but if I was being honest, I wish he wasn't hurting over her anymore. I wished he would give relationships another chance. Because…I think we could be pretty good together.

He leaned over me and kissed me but didn't enter me.

I gripped his back and moved underneath him, wanting to feel him inside me. I was so wet that he wouldn't have a tough time getting past my tightness. But it still didn't come.

He kept kissing me but then that stopped too. He looked down at me, shame in his eyes. "I'm sorry...I can't do this."

Like a wrecking ball had smacked into me, I was floored with disappointment. Everything up to this moment was amazing and hot. But now he wanted to retreat? Now he wanted to stop? "Why?"

He released a deep sigh, which was full of regret. "I don't know...I just can't."

"Are you thinking about her?" The words came out of my mouth without being censored.

"No, not at all," he said. "Just you. I don't know why I can't." He looked away from me, like he couldn't stand to look at me. Then he moved down my body and yanked my hips to the edge of the bed.

"What are you—"

His lips moved to the area between my legs and he kissed me hard like he did before. His tongue did amazing and tantalizing things to me, making me spiral hard and out of control. His tongue did all the right things, circling my clitoris then penetrating hard inside me. I gripped the sheets because it felt so amazing.

I lay back and enjoyed what he was doing. My hands moved into his hair and I pulled him further in between my legs, wanting more. When I looked down at him, his eyes met mine, and a dirty expression was on his face. He used one hand to circle my nub and he used his tongue everywhere else.

I felt the slow burn deep in my stomach and noticed the way it stretched to every other part of my body. It migrated south, and then an amazing orgasm overtook me completely and utterly. I felt like I was having a divine intervention, something out of this world. I writhed on the bed and screamed. I said his name several times, and I think I even called him king.

When I finished and came back to earth, my nipples were hard and I was panting, out of breath. I moved my fingers through my hair, recovering from the insane pleasure I was just given. It was the best head I've ever gotten, hands down.

Troy stood up then leaned over me. "King?" That cocky grin was on his face. "You know, I've been called a lot of things but that has to be the first."

I felt so satisfied I couldn't be embarrassed. "Leave me alone."

He kissed the area between my legs once more. "I love the way you taste. Reminds me of watermelon."

"I have a sweet pussy," I teased.

"The sweetest." He cradled me with one arm then moved me up the bed until my head was on a pillow. Then he got into bed beside me. His arm hooked around my waist like he was ready for bed.

"What?" I asked. "You think I'd leave you hanging like that?"

A grin stretched from ear-to-ear. "I was hoping you wouldn't. But I already left you hanging."

"You faltered but made up for it." I moved over him then took his dick into my mouth again, which was free of the condom.

He lay back on the pillow and groaned. "You sure know how to suck dick."

I pulled him out and jerked him off with my hand. "Thank you."

He grabbed my neck and pulled me down to his head again. He guided me up and down, being more aggressive than before. While our intimacy was gentle and thoughtful, there was obvious heat and chemistry between us. It was an explosive relationship like I'd never had before. Perhaps it was because we were friends, or maybe it was just because he was ridiculously hot. Or maybe it was another reason entirely.

He tapped the side of my head, telling me he was about to come.

I kept going, wanting him to release in my mouth. I knew I came all over his tongue and he should do the same.

He took a deep breath and tensed. "Baby, I'm about to come."

I deep-throated him.

"Fuck." He gripped my neck then released. It was a lot more than I was used to, and I noticed it right in the beginning. It filled my mouth and the back of my throat. I immediately swallowed because it was so much. I kept going until he was completely done, wanting the orgasm to last as long as possible. When he was finished, I pulled away and let his partially hard dick rest on his stomach.

He sighed and closed his eyes. "You really are the perfect woman."

I lay beside him and got comfortable for bed. But the area between my legs burned again. Seeing him come and enjoy my mouth so much got me fired up. I wasn't sure how to tell him that or if I should.

He moved next to me then cuddled with me, his chest pressed to my back. He held me tightly, and his fingers linked with mine over my stomach. He didn't strike me as the cuddling type but I was clearly wrong.

He moved his lips to the back of my neck and kissed me gently.

"Troy?"

"Hmm?" he said quietly.

Should I tell him? I felt a little embarrassed but he said we should always be honest. And it was nice having a fuck buddy that would please me however I wanted. It was the whole reason I agreed to this. "I want you again."

He sat up slightly and leaned over me. "Yeah?" There was an amused look in his eyes.

"Watching you come...got me all excited again."

"I'll always be jealous of females," he said as he opened my legs and moved between them. "I wish I could come twice in a row." He positioned himself then gave me a gentle kiss on the clitoris.

"You don't mind?" Most guys wouldn't even go down on me once.

"I'll eat your pussy as many times as you want. Because I love it."

***

When I woke up the following morning, a big hunky man was wrapped around me. His arms formed steel cages, and his chest was an ironclad wall. His hair was messy from the night before, and a relaxed expression was on his face. One hand was fisted in my hair, and I suspected it'd been there all night.

Before getting up, I stared at him for a long time, noting the handsome features of his perfect face. His dark hair contrasted against his pale face, and his eyes, if they were open, would emit their own glow. I examined his hard jaw and sprinkled a few kisses there. A shadow was already coming in from not shaving, however distant it was.

While I wanted to watch him all morning, I needed to get up and empty my bladder and brush my teeth. Slowly, I slid from his arms, grabbed his shirt off the floor on the way, and then walked out.

As soon as I put his shirt on, it was baggy. It reached my knees and made me feel a million times smaller than I really was. I headed to the bathroom and did my thing before I walked into the kitchen and figured out what to cook my guest for breakfast. All I had was cereal and coffee. Hopefully, that would have to do.

I brewed the coffee then sat at the kitchen table with a magazine. My hair was a mess and all over the place but there was no saving it. I didn't want to take a shower just in case Troy needed to use the restroom when he woke up.

Half an hour later, the door cracked. "There's my teddy bear."

I looked up and smirked at him. He leaned against the doorway wearing his boxers. His perfectly sculpted body got me excited all over again. And I couldn't forget that gorgeous face if I tried. When he smiled, a dimple formed on each cheek. He was the only man I met who could be incredibly sexy and cute at the same time. "Your teddy bear had to pee and make coffee."

"Wow…so she can do more than snuggle." He came out then leaned down and gave me a warm kiss. The embrace was simple but I squeezed my thighs together anyway. Anytime he kissed me, there were sparks deep in my eyes. He eyed my baggy shirt. "I've never seen you look hotter."

"Yeah?"

He kissed my neck. "Yeah." Then he headed to the bathroom. "Mind if I use it?"

"It's all yours."

He walked inside and did his business. But when I heard the faint sound of a toothbrush, I knew he was brushing his teeth. Did he bring a spare? Or was he using mine...?

I pounded on the door. "Please tell me you aren't using my toothbrush."

He opened the door, and even though my toothbrush was in his mouth, he somehow smiled. He spit in the sink and shrugged in guilt. "If I'm eating you out every night, then I'm entitled to use your toothbrush."

"But it's *my* toothbrush."

"So?" He cocked an eyebrow. "You'll suck my dick but won't share a toothbrush with me?"

"Bring your own!"

"I will. Geez."

I growled then walked away.

"I used your razor to shave my face. Hope you don't mind." He shut the door and locked it before I could attack him.

"Asshole!" I returned to the table and read my magazine again.

He came out a few moments later, rubbing his cheek with a smug look. "What's for breakfast, Perfect Ten?"

"Frosted Flakes, Nine Inches."

He made his bowl then sat across from me. "Nine? I thought my nickname was Eight Inches?"

"Well, that doesn't do you justice."

140

A smile accompanied with dimples emerged. "You measured me?"

"Not exactly," I said as I kept flipping through the magazine. "But I can tell."

"Hmm?"

"You've never measured yourself?" I asked incredulously.

"Only losers do that." He shoveled a few bites into his mouth.

"You're going to do it when you get home, aren't you?"

"No..."

I gave him a look of triumph.

He stood up and started looking through my drawers.

"What are you doing? Looking for another toothbrush?"

"A measuring tape."

I rolled my eyes. "Right now?"

He snatched it then closed the drawer. "Found it." He sat down again then touched himself under the table.

I gave him an incredulous look. "At the kitchen table?"

"Now or never, baby." He looked down at himself then turned to me. "Show me your tits so I can get hard."

"No."

"Come on." He nudged me under the table. "Do daddy a favor."

I made a disgusted face. "You can be so sweet then you can be so gross."

"Fine. I'm going to remember the way you gave me head last night...fuck, that was good." He closed his eyes and remained quiet.

"I'm right here..."

He held up a finger. "Shh..."

I sipped my coffee and tried to ignore him.

He opened his eyes a few seconds later. "He's ready."

"Yippie..."

He pulled out the measuring tape then did his business under the table. Then his face broke out in a grin. "What do you know? I am nine inches. Good eye, Perfect Ten."

"I'm so glad I could be of service to you," I said sarcastically.

"Now, how can I get rid of it...?" He rubbed his chin then gave me a meaningful look.

"That was sly."

He released a quick laugh. "Come on. After that amazing blowjob, that's what I'm always thinking about when we're together, just to give you a heads up."

"That's sweet..."

"Hey, you tell me your needs and I'm there. Like last night. And I tell you my needs..."

"Then I want some action when I'm done with you."

He put his hands behind his head. "I'm more than happy to oblige."

***

We were in bed.

Troy wasn't a distant sleeper like most guys. He was all over me, all the time. He stuck to me like a magnet, our bodies tangled together. Our hands were intertwined together like usual.

"You don't strike me as a cuddler," I said.

"I'm not."

"Then why do you do it with me?"

He shrugged. "I like it. I do a lot of things with you and I don't understand why I do them."

"Like what?" I asked.

"Well, I'm still here when I should have left hours ago."

"Why haven't you?"

"I like being with you." He stroked my hair gently. "I was actually going to ask if you wanted to spend the rest of the weekend with me at my beach house—not as a decorator."

"Really?" Excitement pounded in my heart.

"Yeah." His smile stretched when he saw my enthusiasm. "We can hit the beach, have a picnic, do some skinny-dipping..."

"You've already seen me naked. What's so fascinating about being naked in a pool?"

"Your nipples will be hard."

I rolled my eyes. "I would love to—minus the skinny-dipping."

"Cool," he said. "I haven't had anyone over there since I bought it."

"We should invite Rhett and Aspen."

He shrugged. "Then I can't be myself around you." His voice lowered into one of sadness. "And you're the only person I can truly be myself around. I'm not giving that up for anything."

"Yeah?" His words touched my heart in a profound way.

"Yeah."

"I feel the same way."

He rubbed his nose against mine. "I'm going to grab a few things. I'll pick you up in an hour."

"Okay."

***

After we arrived at his beach house, we placed our bags into the bedroom and the snacks in the kitchen. The sun was out and it was a clear day, perfect for sunbathing and swimming.

"I'm so jealous," I said as I grabbed a beach towel from his closet.

"Of what?" His usual cocky smile came in, so I already knew what he was going to say. "My good looks? My charm?" He nodded to his crotch. "The gifts bestowed upon me?"

I walked passed him with the beach towel around my waist. "No, idiot. That you have a beach house."

"Oh." He nodded. "That too."

"I'm surprised you don't live here instead."

He shook his head and put sunblock on his nose. "Not practical. In Manhattan, I can leave my apartment and walk a few steps to twenty different restaurants. There's nothing here but a Taco Bell."

"Hey, Taco Bell is awesome," I said defensively.

"Maybe once in a while. You think I look like this from eating fast food all the time?"

"I'm surprised you can walk through the front door with that big head of yours."

"Which head are you talking about, sweetheart?" A smug look was on his face.

"You're ridiculous." I marched out back then headed to a nice place in the sand. I lay my towel down then lay on my back with sunglasses on. The sun was warm but there was a breeze so I wouldn't fry.

Troy joined me a few moments later. "Popsicle?" He handed it to me.

"Sure." I grabbed it then shoved it into my mouth.

He watched me, making it obvious he was staring.

"What?" I asked.

"I just like to watch you suck things."

I swatted him on the arm gently.

He laughed. "Sorry...couldn't help it."

We lay side-by-side and stared at the surf and waves.

He finished his Popsicle before I did and shoved the wrapper under his towel so it wouldn't fly away. I did the same. Silence ensured for a long time. The sound of seagulls looking for scraps and the crashing waves came to my ears.

"Can I ask you something?" I said.

"Whatever you want." He rested his hands behind his head and lay back.

"Why couldn't you have sex with me?" It'd been on my mind all day. He didn't have a reason for it but that just confused me more. He was hard and I was ready. What stopped him?

"I already told you, Harper. I don't know."

"You can't *not* know."

"It just didn't feel right," he said. "I felt like I was doing something wrong."

"Because I'm not Alexia?" I demanded. I was growing impatient with his weird feelings toward this girl. She left him and broke his heart. Why wouldn't he forget about her already? Why was I so upset about this?

"No." He sat up and looked at me. "I never think about her when I'm with you. Maybe that's why I like to be around you so much. I'm actually happy with you. You keep the bad dreams away. You...fix me."

"I still don't understand..."

"I don't either," he said honestly. "My brother has his theory...I'm not sure if I believe it."

"What?"

"He thinks I can't sleep with a girl unless I'm in love with her. I sincerely hope he's wrong because that would be shitty. He doesn't think it has anything to do with Alexia. I just want that intimacy and happiness back. Lonely nights and meaningless sex aren't enough for me. I don't know what to think."

His words gave me a lot to think about. "What were you like before you met her?"

"I'd fuck any girl, any time. I was the biggest manwhore in Manhattan. But when I met Alexia, all of that changed. I settled down because I thought she was the one. Then she wasn't..."

"You seemed too experienced to only be with one girl your whole life..."

"I've been around," he admitted. "And honestly, despite the way it ended, I liked monogamy. I liked only being with one woman. Our love and physical relationship grew with every passing day. But after she shattered me, I could never do it again. There was a lot of joy in the relationship but there was more pain in the end. Now it's fucked me up in the head and I can't even function right anymore."

"No," I said gently. "I just think you're scared. And there's nothing wrong with that."

"I'm afraid I'm doomed to feel this way forever."

"You are," I said honestly. "If you don't take another chance."

He sighed. "Easier said than done."

'Three years is a long time to be with someone. You don't just get over that in a day or a year."

"How long should it take?" he demanded. "She was with someone a week after we broke up. What hurts more than anything else was the fact we were together and she wasn't happy. I had no idea and she never told me. Honesty would have been much better than the web of lies she created." He dug his toes into the sand and stared at his feet. "Have you been in a serious relationship?"

"No."

"Never?" he asked in surprise.

"Never."

"May I ask why?"

"I just haven't found the right guy. I've dated and had a few flings but that's it."

"Sounds like someone else is scared..." He turned to me with a knowing look.

"No." I pulled my knees to my chest. "I just don't want to waste my time with someone I don't think is going to work. Basically, I'm the opposite of Alexia."

He released a painful laugh. "You couldn't be more different."

"I really think you should try again."

"No," he said firmly. "I'm happy with the way my life is."

"Really?" I challenged. "Because I haven't gotten that impression so far."

"Well, I've been really happy with you..."

When he said things like this, it made me wonder if Troy and I could have something more. The longer I was around him, the more attached I became. I never had trouble guarding my heart or protecting my feelings, but they were spiraling out of control with Troy. I loved spending time with him, and every time he left, I was sad. I thought about him all day at work, and whenever we kissed, it was explosive. I never had that kind of chemistry with anyone else. It was natural with him. Did he not feel it too? Was I the only one? He did warn me not to fall for him. I promised I wouldn't but I was starting to break that promise. "I'm happy with you too."

He stared at the water and rested his arms on his knees.

Since we were always honest with each other, I decided to ask something dangerous. But I didn't see the harm in it. "Could you ever picture yourself with me?" I couldn't be the only person who felt this connection. It had to be mutual. That spark was there from the beginning. It was masked by his cocky attitude but it was there, deep down.

He turned his gaze on me but his eyes were dark. "You're the only woman I could picture myself with, Harper."

***

The weekend at the beach house came and went, and I missed it as soon as we were back in the city. It was

148

nice to be out in the open with the sea just feet away. Troy and I cuddled on the patio furniture, and we watched the ocean while he ran his fingers through my hair. Hours had passed but neither one of us spoke.

But now that vacation was gone.

I had a lot of work to do that week, and a lot of new clients came in. Troy and I had lunch every day, and soon as I was off work, he called me and asked if he could come over. Some evenings he worked, but I never asked him about it. For some reason, knowing he was out with other girls made me uncomfortable. A knot formed in my stomach and made me feel sick.

I was finishing an order with an art company when someone walked inside my office. My secretary spoke to him but I didn't pay much attention. I was still on the phone, and I finished the call before I turned to a potential client.

Troy walked inside, wearing jeans that hung low on his hips and a t-shirt that highlighted his expansive chest. He looked around my office as he walked and nodded in approval. "This place is sweet." He leaned over the desk and kissed me gently on the lips.

My assistant caught the affection then turned away.

"Thanks," I said. "I like it."

"I just realized something," he said. "We're both business owners."

"You own Beautiful Entourage?"

"We're all equal partners in it."

"Oh." I never knew that. "Impressive."

"No, this office is impressive." He looked around again, taking it all in.

"So, what brings you down here?"

149

He stood with his hands in his pockets. "I realized I hadn't seen your office so I wanted to stop by. Plus, I wanted to get lunch with my lady."

My lady? He said he didn't want a girlfriend but sometimes he treated me like I was. "Well, I already have plans."

"What?" He looked devastated. We saw each other every day but that didn't seem to be enough—for both of us. "With who?"

"Aspen."

"Oh..."

"I haven't seen her much. She's been busy with Rhett and I've been busy with you."

"Yeah..." He rubbed the back of his neck. "I haven't been hanging out with Rhett or the guys like I usually do."

"We're terrible friends."

He laughed. "I suppose. But when BJ's are involved, it's understandable."

I shot him a hateful look. "Watch your language when you're in my office." I nodded to my assistant a few feet away.

He eyed her then turned back to me. "You give the best head in the fucking world, Perfect Ten." He didn't yell it but he didn't lower his voice either.

I smacked his arm. "Knock it off or get out."

"How about you get on your knees?"

I smacked him again, this time harder. "Just get out."

"Promise me I'll see you the second you get off work."

"Why?" I asked.

"What do you mean why?" he barked. "Just do it."
He leaned forward and gave me a kiss before he walked
out. The bell rang as the door opened and closed, and soon
the silence of the office descended.

My assistant turned toward me, a grin on her face.
"He's cute."

I rolled my eyes. "He's cocky, that's what he is."

***

When I arrived at the diner, Aspen was there. But
she wasn't alone. Rhett was sitting beside her, and across
the table, was a handsome man I'd never seen before. He
had dark brown hair like Troy and there was a faint scar
along his eyebrow. He was extremely good-looking but in a
dangerous way. I assumed this was one of the six guys who
ran Beautiful Entourage.

"Hey," I said when I approached the booth.

"Hey." Aspen's eyes widened in excitement when
she looked at me. "You look cute."

"You always look cute." I sat in the booth beside the
beautiful stranger.

"She does always look cute." Rhett gave Aspen an
affectionate look.

"Wow," Aspen said. "This lunch is starting off great."

The man extended his large hand to me. "Cato."

I shook it. "Harper."

"I've heard about you." His eyes darkened in
realization. "You've got quite a mouth and you're a hottie."

Did Troy say that?

"That's not what I said," Aspen argued. "I said she's
got sass and she's gorgeous."

"That's what I said," Cato argued.

"You said it in a really crude way," Aspen said.

"Anyway..." Cato turned back to me. "I like blondes."

"Thank you for sharing," I said sarcastically.

He chuckled. "I like you. Most guys like girls who are pushovers. I like them hotheaded and bossy. We'll get along just great."

"Good to know." I waved down the waitress and ordered a coke.

Cato put his arm over the back of my chair. "So...interior decorator?"

"Yep."

"That's pretty cool," he said. "Kudos."

"Thanks."

"You can decorate my bedroom anytime," he said bluntly.

I cocked an eyebrow while I looked at him. "Do you talk to all girls like this?"

"Give her space, man," Rhett said. "When I said I would introduce you, I didn't mean for you to attack her."

"Sorry..." Cato pulled his arm away. "When you walked inside, I didn't expect you to be so hot. I'll back off."

"Thank you." I gave Aspen a glare.

She smiled innocently.

Cato tried talking to me again. "Seriously, my apartment needs to be decorated. It's literally couches and a foosball table. Not very homey or inviting."

"I'm more than happy to help you," I said.

"Troy said you did his beach house," Cato said. "And you did a good job."

"I always do a good job," I argued.

"Sass..." He wore a smug grin. "I like it."

The food arrived and we ate quietly. I found myself talking to Cato more than Aspen and Rhett. Perhaps they did this on purpose. If they did, I'd have to kick some ass.

"We're going out when Aspen gets off work," Cato said. "You should come."

Was he asking me out? This was dangerous. I was seeing Troy secretly so I couldn't tell them that. I wouldn't be doing anything wrong if I went out with Cato but I felt guilty anyway. Troy could never give me something more but that didn't mean I wanted something more from someone else. "Actually, I'm busy tonight..."

"No, she's not," Aspen said quickly. "She'll be there."

I shot her a glare that said, "What the hell are you doing?"

She responded with her own look that said, "This is happening. Do not fight it."

I really didn't have an excuse to get out of this. As far as Aspen knew, I hadn't been seeing anyone for the past two months. It made sense for her to hook me up with a hot guy. And it was totally out of character for me to refuse the idea. I was stuck and had no defense.

"She'll be there," Aspen said.

"Sweet." Cato winked at me. "I'll make sure you have a good time."

"Will you not say cheesy lines, then?"

He laughed. "I'll try."

***

The second I got off work, Aspen walked into my office. She wore a blue dress that was tight on her chest. She looked hot, like usual. "Ready to go?"

I gave her that look that warned her I was about to speak my mind.

"Come on, Cato is really cute. Why wouldn't you want to go out with him?"

I had no excuse. "He's Rhett's friend. Isn't that a conflict of interest?"

She rolled her eyes. "You guys are both adults. You'll be fine."

I wasn't sure why I felt so guilty about this. Troy and I were just friends and I wasn't doing anything wrong. But I felt like I was betraying him anyway.

Aspen spotted my unease. "Give me one good reason why you don't want to go."

"I just...he seems like a manwhore who keeps tally of the chicks he fucks."

"So?" she asked. "When have you ever cared about that? You really need to get out and stop stressing about your sister and her engagement. And when was the last time you'd been with a guy? I'm doing you a favor."

I needed to drop this act otherwise she would know something was off. "You're right."

"I know I am," she said. "Now let's go."

"Right this second?" I asked. I hadn't even had a chance to call Troy and tell him what was going on. "Can I change first?"

"Why?" she asked seriously. "You look great. Your legs look awesome."

A grin stretched my face but I quickly wiped it away. "Well, I need to touch up my make up."

"No," she said. "You'll take an hour and a half. I know you. They are already waiting down at the bar."

I guess I could just text Troy on the way. "Fine." I grabbed my purse and walked out with her.

She moved beside me, her brown hair moving in the breeze from the speed of our walk. "You know, Rhett was a manwhore before we met. He's completely different now."

"Interesting." *Why was she telling me this?*

"Cato might be a little out there but he'd come down to earth if he met the right gal."

"And you think I'm the right gal?" I asked incredulously.

"He said you were hot."

"I would never date an escort," I blurted.

"Why?" she demanded. "There's nothing wrong with it."

"You really don't care that every time Rhett works, he's putting his arm around some girl and she's looking at him like he's the sexiest man she's ever seen? That would get under my skin quick."

"But that happens on a daily basis no matter what he does. Even if he goes to the grocery store women go ga-ga over him."

I pulled out my phone and kept walking. "I'm the jealous type, Aspen. When I have a man, I don't share him with anyone." We were almost to the bar so I sent out a quick message to Troy. *I got caught up in something. I'll let you know when I'm free.*

You better hurry the hell up. My dick misses your mouth.

Even when he said crude things it made me smile.

"What are you smiling about?" Aspen asked.

I returned my phone to my purse. "Nothing."

***

Cato got me another drink then cornered me in the booth. He kept his voice low and pretended the other two weren't even there. "I had a girl ask me to marry her—like actually marry her. She was willing to offer me million to be her real husband for the rest of my life."

Both of my eyebrows shot up. "That's the creepiest thing I've ever heard."

"I know," he said with a laugh. "No amount of money could get me to settle down with a stranger. Fucking psychopath." He drank his beer then regarded me with his green eyes that reminded me of moss on the north side of trees. "I love blondes."

"You already said that."

"I'm saying it again. You're a perfect ten, Harper." His eyes showed his sincerity.

I found it ironic that both Troy and Cato said the same thing. Perhaps Troy talked about me and referred to me that way. It made me feel warm at the possibility.

Cato leaned closer to me like he was going to kiss me.

"Whoa, buddy." I put my hand on his chest and kept him back.

A cocky grin spread across his face. "I promise you won't want to stop once it starts."

"I promise I'll knee you in the balls once it starts."

Instead of being offended, he chuckled lightly. "How many more drinks do I have to buy?"

"None."

"Then let's go in the bathroom," he blurted.

"You think I'll put out for free drinks?"

"I think you'll put out for a real man."

I rolled my eyes. "Does this crap work on other girls?"

He backed off and confusion came into his face. "Yeah..."

"Well, they must be stupid."

"How about you lighten up and give me a real chance?" he asked.

"How about you actually respect me and we'll see?"

"Fine." He leaned back, giving me some space.

"I'm not easy, so if that's what you want, then you're wasting your time."

"I'm not looking for anything," he argued. "You're beautiful and I want to take this wherever it will go— preferably the bathroom stall."

"Smooth..."

He chuckled then clanked his glass against mine. "I like a challenge, Harper. I'm not deterred easily."

The truth was, if Troy weren't in my life, I'd probably go for him. He was too good-looking for his own well being, and he had a playfulness I found attractive. Troy and I were nothing and we never would be, but that would be too awkward to be with Cato. Plus, it just didn't feel right. Anytime Cato came too close to me, Troy came into my mind and I felt like I was betraying whatever I had with Troy—as complicated as that sounded.

Rhett was making out with Aspen when his phone rang. "Hold that thought." He held up his finger then looked at the phone. "This will only take a second." He took the call. "What's up?" He paused. "At the bar with Aspen, Cato, and Harper." He stared at Aspen then snuck a kiss. "Yeah, Harper. Why?"

That caught my attention. *Was he talking to Troy?*

"We'll be here for a while so come down whenever. Bye." He hung up.

Shit, was that Troy? That would be awkward.

"Who was that?" Aspen asked.

"Troy," Rhett answered.

Fuck.

"Cool," Aspen said.

"Hopefully, he finds a date," Cato said. "Because I'm busy with this fine number over here."

I glared at him. "This fine number has a name."

"Harper," he said. "My apologies."

How would I explain to Troy what was going on? I didn't want him to think I was voluntarily dating his friend. Or maybe he wouldn't care at all. He didn't have any deep feelings for me other than friendship. Maybe it wouldn't make a difference to him. But if it didn't, that would hurt more than I would ever admit.

Troy

Why were the four of them at a bar? Two guys and two girls? That sounded like a double date. Or maybe I was overanalyzing it. Why would Harper go out with Cato? He didn't seem like her type. But then again, I didn't know what her type was. I always thought—hoped—it was me.

I walked inside and found their table. To my horror, Cato's entire body was turned toward Harper and he had her backed up into a wall. He was smiling while he spoke to her, and it was clear he was giving her his best moves. I'd known him long enough to understand when he was hitting on a girl, even from afar.

Pain suddenly landed on my shoulders and I felt sick. Betrayal and hurt washed through me. I thought Harper was mine but she preferred someone else. She didn't even tell me about it. It was Alexia all over again...

I stood there, unable to move or think. But then I realized something. Harper wasn't my girlfriend. She was just a friend I was seeing casually. There was nothing meaningful between us and I never wanted there to be. So why was I so devastated by this? Why was I so hurt? Why did it remind me so much of Alexia?

"Are you just going to stand there or actually join us?" Rhett asked when he spotted me.

I snapped out of my moment and pretended I was perfectly fine. In reality, a small part of me just died. "What's up?" I pulled up a chair and sat at the end of the booth. I purposely didn't look at Harper, unable to fight the hurt I felt.

Cato turned away from Harper to look at me. "You look like hell."

I really wanted to rip his face off. He was way too close to Harper and I didn't like it one bit. Jealousy coursed through me and I wanted to break every bone in his body. Then I wanted to cut off his dick so he wouldn't be able to put it anywhere near Harper. "Go fuck yourself."

"Whoa..." Cato raised both hands. "Damn, did you have a bad day or something?"

"Or something." I still didn't look at Harper.

"Everything alright, man?" Rhett asked as he patted my shoulder.

I pushed it off in a defensive way. "I'm just...stressed out."

"About?" Aspen asked.

"One of my clients..." That was all I could say.

"Nate's parents still won't come around?" Rhett questioned.

"Yeah." That seemed believable enough.

Harper looked at me, and I could feel her gaze penetrate into my skin. "Hey, Troy."

I kept my eyes glued out the window. "Hey."

"Dude," Cato snapped. "I know you're having a bad day but don't take it out on my date."

"Your date?" I hissed. "She's *not* your date." My voice came out so venomous I couldn't believe it.

"Why don't you just go home since you're such unbearable company?" Cato asked. "Because being a shithead isn't suitable to you." He turned to Harper. "Let's dance, baby."

What the fuck did he just call her?

Cato stood up then pulled Harper with him.

She turned to me when we were close together. An apologetic look was on her face.

That didn't mean shit to me.

They walked away and joined the dance floor. I tried not to look but it took all my strength not to. Why was Harper with him? She was way too good for him. He didn't respect her the way I did. He didn't care about her like I did. She was too good for me as it was, but she was better than every guy in that bar.

"You okay, man?" Rhett asked.

"Fine." My strength broke down and I looked at the dance floor. Cato was dancing close with Harper, and they were swaying together with the music. I wanted to vomit. When Cato hugged her waist and pulled her close to his chest, I wanted to flip the table over. Without thinking, I stood up and marched over there.

"What's he doing?" Aspen asked Rhett.

"I haven't got a clue," Rhett said.

I reached the dance floor and moved through the crowd. When Harper was just a foot away, I grabbed her wrist and yanked her away from Cato. She flew into my chest and hit me hard.

"What the fuck are you doing?" Cato demanded.

"My turn." I pulled Harper with me and found a place a few feet away. Then I pulled her to me and danced with her slowly. But the anger coursed through my limbs when I looked at her. The sense of betrayal wouldn't go away. "What the fuck? Why are you with him?"

"Let me explain," she said quickly. "I was dragged into this."

"*Dragged*?" I asked incredulously.

"Aspen set us up and I didn't have a choice. And if I refused, she would know something was off. I couldn't tell her about us. It would be too difficult to explain and it makes me sound pathetic. What other choice did I have?"

"Not date Cato."

"Look, it's just for tonight. I'm not going to go out with him again."

That calmed me down. "You aren't?"

"No, of course not." Her eyes softened when she looked at me.

I realized how crazy I was being. I was acting like a psychopath. "I'm sorry...I don't know what overcame me."

"It's okay."

"Promise me it's just for tonight." I watched her face as I waited for her reaction.

"Promise."

"I don't want to share you with anyone." I stared at her and restrained myself from kissing her. I wanted that comfort of our two lips combining together. I wanted to hold her and never let go.

"I don't want to be shared with anyone."

"Get through the rest of the night. But you're coming home with me."

"That sounds nice."

I stared at her for several heartbeats before I reluctantly let her go. "I'll let you get back to Cato…"

"Okay." Sadness was in her eyes, like she didn't want me to leave her.

I wanted to crush my mouth against hers and claim her for everyone to see, but I managed not to. Without another word, I walked away and returned to the booth where Rhett and Aspen watched me.

I sat down and released a deep sigh. My eyes didn't turn to the dance floor again. Just because Harper didn't like Cato didn't mean I could stand to watch him touch her. It made me sick.

Rhett watched me carefully. "Everything alright?"

"Yeah." I crossed my arms over my chest and looked out the window.

"Are you sure…?" Rhett pressed.

"I said I was fine," I barked.

"Do you have a thing for Harper?" Aspen asked.

I wanted to admit the truth and say I did. I didn't want to hide Harper and share her with my friend. And that scared me. I wasn't ready for another relationship and I didn't think I could ever trust someone to try again, but the idea of Harper being with anyone else….made me want to die. "No."

"Then what was that about?" Aspen asked.

I turned to her. "I've known Cato for a long time. I know what kind of guy he is. Harper needed to know the truth. I care a lot about her."

Aspen seemed to believe me. "She's a big girl, Troy. She can take care of herself.

I wanted to take care of her.

163

***

We migrated toward the bar an hour later and ordered our drinks. Cato was talking quietly with Harper, and they were paired off like a couple. I tried not to watch them but I couldn't help it. I hated the way Cato eye-fucked her. It made my head want to explode.

Rhett and Aspen were just as invested in one another. I felt like a third wheel. Normally, I would pick up a girl in this situation, but the only girl I wanted to pick up was with another guy.

I scanned the bar and tried to find something to entertain myself. I didn't want to stick out like a sore thumb by standing alone but there were only so many things I could do.

When I spotted someone I recognized, I felt sick to my stomach. Stress weighed on my shoulders, and I hated the fact she still instilled this pain within me. I suddenly felt like a coward, wanting to run and hide. I hated looking at her. The last time we spoke, my hatred only increased. There was no bottom to the depth of my despise. "Fuck...you've got to be kidding me." She was going to see me stand alone like a loser. My friends were paired off and I was left out. And the fact she was holding hands with some guy didn't make me feel better.

"What?" Rhett turned to me.

What the fuck should I do? I wanted to get out of there as quickly as possible. I didn't want her to see me. I didn't want her to see the hurt on my face. I didn't want her to know I was still hurting over her even after all this time. "Alexia, she's coming this way." I started to panic. I could turn around and face the bar but she would probably still recognize me.

Harper ended her conversation with Cato and looked in the direction I was staring.

"Stand your ground and pretend to be indifferent," Rhett said. "She doesn't exist."

I was sick of running into her all the time. Would I ever be free? I didn't know what to say to her if she spoke to me. I didn't want to stand here alone and pretend to be confident. My will was slipping away.

She was just a few feet away, and there was nowhere for her to go except right in front of me. I'd have to stand next to her and her boyfriend and not think about the relationship we had that ended with the destruction of my soul.

Harper quickly moved in front of me then stood on her tiptoes. She wrapped her arms around my neck then kissed me hard on the mouth, right in front of everyone we knew.

My body immediately responded, feeling safe in her arms. Alexia faded from my mind once Harper's lips were pressed to mine. All I felt was joy and security. Harper was the one person who understood me. I felt safe with her, complete. Our tongues danced together and I forgot about everyone else in that bar. There was only she and I. Now I didn't give a damn about Alexia and her boyfriend. How could I regret what happened when it led me to Harper? She was the coolest chick I've ever known, and her beauty triumphed over everyone else's. I held her close to me and deepened my kiss. Harper was the only thing that mattered to me.

I broke our kiss and didn't search for Alexia. All I cared about was Harper. "You want to get out of here?"

"Yes, please."

***

"People are going to wonder what's going on between us," Harper said as she lay beside me in bed.

We fooled around and found each other's release but I still couldn't do the deed. I wanted to, but as we fooled around, something held me back, again. I didn't know what it was. "We'll just tell them you kissed me to help me out. Then we walked out to get me out of the situation."

"Do you think she saw?" Her leg was wrapped around my hip and her hands rested on my chest.

"I don't know," I said. "I didn't look. But she probably did."

"Does that give you any satisfaction?" she asked.

"Not really," I admitted. "I just don't want her to think I'm alone when she's moved on with other guys. When I saw her at the grocery store, I purposely put four boxes of condoms in my cart when I was talking to her just to make a statement."

"Four?" She nodded slowly. "Wow. That's a lot of sex."

I rolled my eyes. "I know. It's lame."

"No, it's not lame," she said gently. "I'd probably do something similar."

"No, you're stronger than I am. You wouldn't have cared at all."

"But I've never been in a three-year relationship," she reasoned. "You really shouldn't be so hard on yourself."

"I'm pathetic, Harper," I said sadly. "Denying it doesn't make me feel any better." I turned on my back and faced the ceiling.

She cuddled into me and rested her head on my chest. "You were really mad when you saw me with Cato."

Silence echoed in the room. I remembered how mad I was and how much I wanted to break Cato's legs. "Sorry about that."

"You felt betrayed, didn't you?" Her voice carried her understanding.

"Honestly, yeah...I'm not sure why."

She propped her elbow and rested her head on her palm. "I felt terrible for hurting you. I would never date Cato. And when I was dragged into the situation, I just wanted to get out."

"I've never been so jealous in my life." I didn't know what it meant. Was I just insecure? Was I just protective of Harper? What did that mean?

"Why?" she whispered.

"I really don't know, Harper. I wish I did."

She rubbed my chest then kissed the skin over my heart. Her hair moved across my skin, touching me lightly and making me feel calm. She kissed the area again then moved her lips to mine.

I wanted to stay like this forever. I really didn't know how I felt or what everything meant, but I knew something else was between us. I couldn't put my finger on it and neither could she. But I knew one thing.

I didn't want to share her with anyone.

Harper

When Aspen walked into my office, I immediately knew why she was there. That kiss with Troy wouldn't go overlooked, and she probably went by my apartment later that night and realized I wasn't there. Where else would I be except with Troy?

She approached my desk with a knowing look in her eyes. "Lunch?"

"Do I have a choice?"

"Nope."

I sighed then saved the document on my computer. "Where do you want to go?"

"It doesn't matter to me." Her voice was clipped, like she was angry or disappointed in me. She was probably hurt I didn't tell her about Troy. And it was understandable.

I grabbed my purse. "How about Chinese?"

"Whatever." She never said that.

I let the comment slide.

Together, we left and walked a few blocks to the Chinese place we always went to. The silence was awkward, and Aspen clearly wasn't going to speak until she had me cornered at a table. I went through her words in my mind, anticipating what she might say or do. But in the end, I didn't really care. I didn't like lying and I was terrible at it.

Once we got a table and ordered our waters, Aspen pounced.

"How long has it been going on?"

The smart thing would be to lie about the whole thing. I already had a cover story in mind but I didn't want to use it. Aspen was my best friend and it felt wrong to mislead her. "About two months."

"Why didn't you tell me?" Hurt was in her voice.

"Because it's not what you think."

"How do you mean?"

I took a deep breath before I explained everything to her.

"So, he's using you to get over Alexia, and you're using him to pretend to be your boyfriend to your family?"

"Yeah."

"And you're sleeping with him?"

"Actually...no. We haven't slept together."

Aspen seemed more confused. "Okay..."

"Every time we're about to do it he chickens out. He doesn't understand why, but his brother thinks Troy can't be with someone else unless he's in love with them. That's why he's struggling so much. I'm starting to believe the same thing."

"But you guys do other things?" she asked.

"Yeah. And we spend a lot of time together. Actually, I see him almost every day. He's quickly become my best friend, and I can't remember the last time I slept alone."

She studied me for a long time, her thoughts unguarded. "You've fallen for him, haven't you?"

I knew it was written all over my face. I was shocked Troy hadn't picked up on it. It was something I didn't expect to happen. There were a lot of things about him I didn't like, but the things I did like about him I loved. "Yeah..."

"Be careful, Harper," she said. "You're already in so deep."

"I know. But call me crazy, I think he feels the same way."

"He seemed pretty upset when he ran into Alexia the other night," she reasoned.

"He was," I agreed. "But I don't think he misses her. I think he just fears what she represents—pain. And he got so jealous when he thought I was with Cato."

"That's true."

"And he's said things to me..."

"Like what?" she asked.

"That I'm the only woman he can picture himself with. That he's never been so jealous in his life. That I'm his best friend and the only person who understands him..." In my heart, I thought there was a real possibility that Troy felt what I did. It wasn't just a fantasy anymore. It was a real possibility. We could have what I wanted to have. But he just needed a little more time to figure it out.

"He really said that?" she asked.

I nodded.

"Maybe you should talk to him. Tell him how you feel."

"He needs more time, and he needs to realize it on his own. If and when he does sleep with me, I'll talk to him then."

"That makes sense." She still seemed down, hurt.

"I'm sorry I didn't tell you. Troy and I were supposed to be a short-term fling but it just went haywire. I never anticipated I would feel this way about him. He's a cocky asshole on the outside, but when I got to know him underneath, I realized he was nothing like that. He's actually...pretty amazing."

Aspen's hurt aura disappeared, and a smile stretched her lips. "I'm happy for you."

"I wouldn't say that yet..."

"Rhett only says amazing things about Troy, so I think you're right to assume he's a great person. Men aren't as clear-minded as women. I'm sure Troy does feel the same way about you, but he might not realize it. And I think it's smart to wait until he figures it out on his own. Otherwise, it might just push him away."

"Exactly," I said.

"How amazing would it be if you and Troy got married and me and Rhett got married?" She squirmed in her seat in excitement.

"Let's not get carried away..."

"But wouldn't that be amazing!"

"It would." I entertained the idea for a moment and felt a thrill shoot up my spine. Just staying at Troy's beach house with him was my idea of a fantasy. Lying together in bed after making love and whispering words of devotion was what I craved. When I realized the extent of my feelings, the weight of reality set on my shoulders.

I was in love with Troy.

How did that happen?

Troy

I was getting my files at Beautiful Entourage when Cato walked inside.

"Dude, what the hell?"

I grabbed my things and didn't look at him.

"If you had a thing for Harper, you should have told me. I wouldn't have gone for her if I'd known."

I couldn't look at him so I shoved everything under my arm and headed for the door.

"Talk to me, man." He grabbed the folders and yanked them out of my grasp.

I turned to him, threatening him with my beady eyes. "Get off my ass, Cato."

"No. I want to talk about this."

"Are we girls now?" I hissed.

"I just don't want you to be pissed at me. I know the rules. I would never go for your girl. I just didn't know she was your girl. You never told me that."

I knew Cato was getting the short stick of the situation. "I'm not pissed at you."

"Fooled me," he said. "You can barely look at me."

"I'm just a little worked up over it," I admitted. "I didn't like watching you eye-fuck her."

Cato released a frustrated sigh. "Again, I didn't know. I'm sorry, okay?" He handed the folders back to me.

I took them. "Okay."

"Okay?" he asked. "Does that mean we're cool?"

"Yeah," I said with a nod.

He breathed a sigh of relief. Then a stupid grin stretched his face. "So...you and Harper, huh?"

"Don't start that shit," I said immediately.

"Come on," he said. "I tell you about all my girls and you tell me yours. Why is Harper different?"

"Because she is," I said firmly.

Rhett opened the door and walked inside. When he saw us talking, a grin stretched on his face. "Fighting over Harper?"

"There's nothing to fight about," I said calmly.

Rhett joined the circle but stood close to Cato, like he was taking his side.

I felt outnumbered.

"So...what's with you and Harper?" Rhett asked. "I distinctly remember you saying there was nothing going on. You lied to me?" The hurt of my betrayal was in his voice.

"I didn't lie...exactly."

"Then what did you do, *exactly*?" he snapped.

I didn't mind explaining it to Rhett but not in Cato's presence. Rhett was the only one who knew about my feelings toward Alexia. "Can we talk about this later?" I glanced at Cato.

"No, we're talking about this now." Rhett grabbed my arm and pulled me outside. When we were in the alleyway, he stared me down. "Now spit it out."

I organized my thoughts then explained everything to him.

"That has to be the most fucked up thing I've ever heard," Rhett snapped. "You're sleeping with Harper to get over Alexia?"

"But I haven't slept with her," I argued. "I just can't do it. I care about her too much. I can't fuck her."

The look in his eyes changed. "I got the distinct impression that you felt something strong for her the other night. I really thought you were going to break Cato's arm."

"I wanted to break both of them, actually."

He crossed his arms over my chest and gave me that look that told me to continue speaking.

"I love being with her. She's like my best friend. I think about her all day, and when I'm finally with her, I'm happy. She's so cool, and she's gorgeous. It's like...I can't even explain it."

"It sounds like you're in love with her." There was a grin on his face.

"But I'm not," I argued. "I'm not over Alexia."

He sighed. "Troy, you *are* over her."

"Then why do I hate her so much? Why do I freak out anytime I run into her? I dream about proposing to her before she throws me off a cliff. Obviously, I'm not over her."

"When you're with Harper, do you think about her?" he asked.

"No," I said immediately. "But when I'm with you, I don't think about her either. That doesn't mean anything."

"Don't you think you're just bitter about the break up? That doesn't mean you still love her."

"But it might," I argued. "How can I be in love with Harper if I feel this way? And I can't offer her anything anyway. I don't do relationships and I never will. The end."

"You really don't think it will be different with Harper?"

I shrugged. "It's not worth the risk. Alexia hurt me a lot. I don't know what I would do if I lost Harper... At least this way she'll always be in my life."

He rubbed the back of his neck. "You're wrong about that."

"How do you mean?"

"When you don't give her what she wants, she's going to find it elsewhere. She's a pretty girl and has a lot of admirers. Can you really stand by and watch her be with someone else? When you could have her if you wanted to?"

The idea of anyone touching her but me sent me into a frenzy. Jealousy coursed through me and I felt sick to my stomach. Harper was my world and I didn't want to share her with anyone. But I couldn't risk my heart again, not like that. "I'd let her go..."

"I don't believe that."

"Well, it's the truth," I said sadly. "I want to keep this relationship with Harper as long as I can. And if she wants to leave...I won't stop her."

"Even after everything you've been through?" he asked incredulously. "You just told me this girl is your best friend, that when you aren't with her all you can think about is the next time you see her. You would really throw that away?"

"She'll just throw me away sometime down the road," I argued.

"No, she won't," he said firmly.

"All relationships end one way or another," I said. "Whether it's through heartbreak or death. I don't want to deal with that pain anymore."

"So, does that mean you don't want a relationship with me?" he challenged.

I didn't understand his meaning. "You're a good-looking guy, Rhett. But you aren't my type..."

He didn't look amused. "We aren't romantically involved but we have a relationship. I love you and you love me. So, when I die, it's going to hurt you. Or are you telling me you're going to be so numb from any emotion that you just won't care about anyone? Troy, that's no way to live. We love people and we lose them. You can't stop living because of it."

"It's not the same thing..."

"I'm your best friend, so you must love me more or equally to the woman you fall in love with. I love Aspen with everything that I have, but I also love you. If I lost either one of you the reaction would be exactly the same. But that's going to stop me from caring about both of you."

I raised my hand. "I know what you're trying to do—"

"And I know you're being an idiot," he snapped. "Tell Harper how you feel and give it a chance. You'll regret it if you don't." He gave me one final look before he walked away and left me standing there alone.

***

I walked into Harper's apartment without knocking. "Baby, it's me."

"I'll be there in a second," she called from the bedroom.

I don't know when I started calling her baby. It just came out.

Harper came out of the bedroom wearing jeans and a tight blouse.

"You look hot," I blurted.

"You always look hot." She wrapped her arms around my neck and gave me a warm greeting.

"Well, I try…"

She slapped my arm playfully. "Why are you always so full of yourself?"

"I have plenty of reasons to be full of myself." I rubbed my nose against hers. "Can I take you out to dinner?"

"You always take me out to places. How about I take you out?" She lowered her arms and grabbed her purse.

"Miss independent…"

"You never let me pay for anything. Let me get this one."

I wrapped my arms around her again and smothered her with kisses. "Someone wants me to do something special tonight…"

She leaned her head back and gave me access to her throat. "No. All I have to do is ask."

I kept kissing her and felt my dick grow hard. "Now I just want to stay in and order a pizza."

"That doesn't sound so bad."

I grabbed her ass and lifted her before I carried her to bed. "Did Aspen harass you today?"

"Yes. Did Rhett?"

"Yes," I answered. "What did you say?"

She flinched for a moment. "What we agreed on. You?"

I didn't want to tell her all the things Rhett said to me, that I might be in love with her and I should give her a chance. I didn't want to get her hopes up if she felt the same way. That would make me feel like a bigger jackass than I already was. "I said the same."

She nodded but there seemed to be distant look of depression in her eyes. She kept her arms wrapped around me and held me closer. Then she locked her lips to mine as I laid her on the bed. We didn't speak for the rest of the night. Instead, we spoke with our bodies.

***

I grabbed a mocha with soy from Starbucks then headed to her office. I knew she got out of bed at the latest time possible so she never grabbed coffee on the way. Instead, she had the crappy stuff at her office. It tasted like dead plants.

I walked inside then headed to her desk. She was typing on her computer, and her long blonde hair stretched down her back. When she recognized my presence, she turned to me. "What a pleasant surprise."

"I was in the neighborhood so I thought I'd bring you a coffee."

She eyed it for a moment then looked up at me, almost surprised. "That was nice of you..."

"It has soy in it. Don't worry."

She took a sip. "And it's delicious. Way better than the crap we have here."

"Well, it's your office," I teased.

"I have more important things to do than focus on getting better coffee."

I leaned over the desk and kissed her like usual. This time when I pulled away, she had a different look in her eyes. I couldn't describe it because I wasn't sure what I was seeing. Harper and I had been different ever since that night in the bar. Our relationship was better, but it was also...different.

"What are you doing today?" she asked.

"I have to work tonight," I said. "Other than that, nothing."

She nodded then pulled out a few papers from her drawer.

"I wished you worked at night so we could see each other during the day. I hate being at home when you're at work."

She opened the folder and didn't say anything.

"Is there something wrong...?"

"No." She turned her eyes back to me but they seemed distant, almost hurt.

"What happened to not lying to each other?"

She sighed then turned to her secretary. "Could you excuse us for a moment?"

"Of course." She grabbed her coffee then walked outside.

I turned back to Harper, wanting to know what she had to say.

Her voice came out strong. "You want to see me all the time. You come to my work and bring me coffee, getting my complicated order exactly right, and you want to spend every waking moment with me." She stared at me like she was finished, like that explained everything.

"Yeah...?"

She grew frustrated. "And I'm jut a friend to you? Because you don't act like it, Troy. You act like I mean a lot more to you, and it's confusing me..."

"Does it bother you?"

"No, of course not. I just...you say you can't have something more with me but you treat me like I'm your girlfriend."

I didn't know what to say. I'd never given much thought to my actions. I just did and said what I wanted to do and say. "You're my friend and I love spending time with you. You've become my best friend...I'm not thinking when I do anything. I just do it."

"And you don't feel anything more for me?"

I wasn't sure. Sometimes I thought I did. Sometimes I didn't. "Why are you asking?"

She looked down at her hands and remained quiet. She pressed her lips firmly together then licked them with her tongue. "Sometimes I think you're in love with me but you're in denial about it." Her voice shook, like she was afraid to say those words. And it seemed like she regretted saying them.

Her words caught me off guard, and they entered one ear and went out the other. A slight sense of panic overcame me. Rhett's words came back to me, and now Harper was saying the same ones. I sunk into the chair facing her desk and felt all the happiness disappear from my body. "Harper, I never want to be in a relationship again. I told you this from the beginning."

She stared at me with a blank expression.

"That hasn't changed and it never will."

"You didn't answer my question."

"I did," I said. "I can't be anything more with you."

"So, you aren't in love with me?" Her voice faltered.

"No..."

"And you being sweet to me and acting like a perfect boyfriend...what does that mean?"

I shrugged. "Nothing..."

She nodded and took a deep breath.

Was she in love with me? Did I give her the wrong impression? Did I hurt her? I'd kill myself if I did. "If this is too hard for you, maybe we should stop seeing each other..." I didn't want that to happen. *At all.* But I couldn't hurt her anymore. I refused to be the person who cause her pain.

"And that would be so easy for you?" she asked quietly.

"It wouldn't be easy...no," I said. "But, I want to do what's best for you."

"You're what's best for me," she whispered. She didn't look at me as she said it.

I walked in there expecting one thing. Instead, I was letting her go. It came out of nowhere, and now pain shot through me in heartfelt waves. I couldn't stop thinking about her that morning and just wanted to bring her coffee. Now I was walking away from her. My heart hurt more than it ever had. "Harper, are you in love with me?"

She wouldn't meet my gaze. "No."

"Then what's the problem?" I whispered.

"I'm not in love with you. But I'm falling in love with you." She moved her eyes to mine, and they were full of emotion. "If you don't want to see me anymore, that's fine. But I find it hard to believe that I'm experiencing all these emotions while you're completely unaware of them. You've built defenses around your mind that are so strong that nothing can penetrate them. You don't even understand what you feel. You can't live in fear forever, Troy. If you gave love a chance again, I promise you it would be different."

I rubbed the back of my neck and considered her words. They went straight into my heart and shattered into indefinite pieces. "Sometimes I think I can...but I can't, Harper. That's not fair to you."

She looked away again. "So, this is it, then?"

I didn't want it to be the end. It was so sudden and unexpected. What would I do without her? What would my life be like? The past two months with her had been wonderful. It was the first time I felt alive in forever. And now I was about to walk away. "I guess..."

She nodded and adopted an indifferent façade. "Take care, Troy. I hope you find...whatever it is you're looking for." All emotion was gone from her face. I felt like we were having a business meeting. It didn't even feel like we were friends anymore.

"Okay..." I stood up and felt weak. My knees were about to give out. I was out of place and lost. The second I severed Harper from my body I didn't feel like myself. It was like I lost an arm or a leg. Without looking back, I walked out, feeling my heart sink further into my stomach.

***

Even days later, I didn't know what to do with myself. Every time I heard a funny joke, I wanted to call Harper and share it. But then I realized she wasn't in my life anymore.

She wasn't even my friend.

My sadness quickly turned to depression, and I found myself going to my beach house more often, just sitting alone and staring into the ocean. Whenever I slept in the bed I shared with her, she was all I could think about. Sometimes her scent was still on the sheets. It was hard to sleep without her in my arms. When I was with Alexia, I never cuddled with her. It was too hot and uncomfortable. But with Harper, I was cold when she wasn't snuggled into my side.

But now she was gone.

She came to me in my dreams, that beautiful smile and soft hair accompanying her. Most of the time, she and I were just sitting together on the beach. Sometimes my dreams were sexual, and I fucked her so hard I broke the bed. And other times, I was down on one knee with a ring in my hand.

I didn't know what to make of it.

But I was doing the right thing by staying away from her. She said she was falling in love with me. A part of me felt warm at the thought, but another part felt terrible. How did this happen? When did it happen? We agreed to just be friends. I would escort her and she would help me move on from Alexia. I couldn't figure it out.

She said she thought I felt the same way but I was in denial about it. Was that true? Was it possible? Harper was special to me. I did think about her all the time, and when I wasn't with her, I wanted to be. But if I were in love with her, wouldn't I have slept with her? If that were the case, why was I holding back?

I couldn't figure it out.

***

Around midnight, I was lying in bed unable to sleep. Sleep was a luxury I didn't enjoy very often anymore. With

185

Harper, I slept like a baby. I was never more rested or satisfied as I was when I was with her.

And not having her there was like not giving enough oxygen. I had just enough to get by, but not enough to be comfortable.

My phone rang on my nightstand and my heart immediately kicked into overdrive. Was it Harper? I used all my restraint not to call her or text her. There were so many times I wanted to do it but I held myself back. Hopefully, she cracked. I desperately wanted to talk to her.

But it was a number I didn't recognize.

Why would a person be calling me at this hour? It was odd. I answered it because I was curious. Maybe it was a friend calling for a ride since they were drunk and they were borrowing someone's phone. "Hello?"

"Mr. Sexton?" It was a male voice, professional. I could tell the man was middle age just by listening to him.

"This is he." My voice was strong but I couldn't deny the fear in my heart. "Who's this?"

"I'm Dr. Palacos," he explained. "From New York Medical Center."

My heart fell into my chest. *Oh shit.*

"Your brother Kyle is in ICU. You're listed as next of kin. I just wanted to let you know he was here."

The room started to spin and my chest constricted. I sat up so quickly that I almost fell over. I gripped the sheets like they would give me strength. "Is he okay?"

"He's doing well. I suspect he'll have a full recovery."

That didn't make me feel better. "What happened?"

"According to a witness, he was taken into an alleyway where five men beat him savagely. He said it was a hate crime because your brother is a homosexual." He said this with no emotion. He was practically a robot.

"Shit," I blurted.

"He's pretty banged up and he has a broken arm but there's no permanent damage. You should come down and see him."

"I'm on my way." I hung up without saying goodbye.

***

When I located his room, Mark was already there. He was at his bedside, holding Kyle's hand. His eyes were red and puffy like he'd been crying just a few minutes ago.

I stopped and stared at my brother, seeing him in a cast with a bunch of tubes hooked up to his body. The reality hit me violently, right in the heart. "Oh my god..."

Mark stood up then hugged me hard. "He's going to be okay. It's hard to see though..." He patted me on the back then pulled away. "He'll be alright. He will, Troy."

Like in a trance, I moved from his arms then approached Kyle. His eyes were closed and he breathed at a steady rhythm. My hand immediately found his and I gripped him tightly. "I'm here, Kyle." My voice came out weak.

Mark moved back to his seat and stayed by Kyle's side. He grabbed Kyle's other hand and released a deep sigh.

I stood over my brother and felt my eyes burn with tears. "Why would someone do this...?"

"I don't know," he whispered.

"Where were you?" I tried to make my voice not sound accusatory.

"Home. He went out with some friends. It must have happened when he was walking home."

"How'd they know he was gay?"

"I have no idea," he said. "But sometimes you can just tell. Maybe it was the way he walked...I don't know."

I sat down and kept my hold on my brother's hand.

"I was going to call your parents but...I didn't know if I should."

I nodded. "Yeah..." *Should I call?* I pulled out my phone but there was one person I needed more than anyone. Only she could help me right now. I called her without thinking about it, and she answered like she'd been waiting for my call.

"Hello?" Her voice came out strong, not like she'd just been sleeping.

"Harper?" My voice was weak and shaky. I couldn't keep the tears out.

"Troy?" Alarm came into her voice. "What's wrong?"

"Kyle is in the hospital...some guys dragged him into the alleyway and...." I couldn't finish my sentence. "I'm at New York Medical Center—"

"I'm coming," she said immediately. "I'll be right there."

She didn't even make me ask. "Thank you."

"Hold on, okay?"

"Okay."

***

Harper came into the room breathing hard like she'd run the whole way. She did make it under seven minutes, so I suspected she had. As soon as I looked at her, I couldn't keep my emotion in check. My eyes started to water with tears, and I stood up so I could fall into her embrace and feel safe.

When Harper looked at me, those beautiful blue eyes no longer looked hypnotic. They were the gates to her soul, and they burned with pain and agony. She mirrored my sorrow, and I could tell she hurt for me.

I moved into her arms and held her as close as possible. My chin rested on her head and I squeezed her hard, using her as a safeguard. My chest rose and fell deeply as the emotion hit me hard. My brother would be okay, but that didn't take away my pain. Someone hurt him when he didn't deserve it. I wish I were there so I could have protected him. He shouldn't have been dragged into an alleyway because of whom he loved. It was just wrong.

Harper pulled away slowly then cupped my face. She wiped my tears away with the pads of her thumb. Then she kissed me gently on the lips, giving me strength when I thought I couldn't find anything. "Is he going to be okay?"

I nodded. "The doctor said he will recover. He has a broken arm and a few bruises but..."

"He shouldn't have to go through it to begin with."

I was grateful she understood me. "Yeah."

She kissed me again, and the touch soothed me. "I'm here for you."

"Thank you." Gratitude came from deep within my heart. She didn't understand what that meant to me.

She took my hand and walked to my brother's side. She stared down at him then brushed his hand with hers. "You look just like him."

"I know." I finally stopped crying and wiped my tears away.

"I'm Mark." He extended his hand to shake Harper's. "I'm Kyle's boyfriend."

"It's nice to meet you." She returned the embrace then rested her hand on Kyle's arm. "I know you can hear us, and know that we're here for you. You aren't alone."

Her words meant a lot to me. I was glad I didn't have to do this alone. And there was only person I could get through the experience with.

***

I didn't want to call my parents. Not because they would overreact and scream. Not because they would cry and make me feel terrible. It was because I feared they wouldn't care. And that would just make this night even more unbearable. When Kyle woke up, what would I say? That Mom and Dad still couldn't stand him because he was gay? Even though he almost died? How could I possibly say that to him?

"Are you going to call?" Mark whispered.

I sighed deeply before I nodded. I pulled out my phone and made the call. With every ring, I hoped they wouldn't answer. But they did.

"Hello?" It was my Dad. "Troy, it's late. Are you okay?"

"No, I'm not," I said firmly.

"What is it, son? Do you need help?"

"Kyle is in the hospital," I said flatly. "He was just jumped. He has a broken arm and a lot of damage. He's in the ICU."

There was a long pause of silence.

"Dad?"

"I told you this would happen. He can't choose this lifestyle and expect to be accepted by society." He almost sounded bored.

My chest started to expand drastically and my palms were sweaty. Anger flushed through me with the power to move mountains. "So, you're saying he deserves this?" I almost couldn't say the words.

"Of course, not," he said. "I'm just saying...it was the risk he took."

I couldn't hold back my anger. "What does it matter? He's your son and he needs you." My eyes started to water again. "Kyle is a good person and you should love him no matter what."

"When he comes to his senses, we'll talk."

I couldn't believe this was real. I couldn't believe these soulless people. How could someone turn their back on their son like this? "When your day comes, and you're sitting in a hospital bed alone, do not expect me to come and wait by your side. When they put you in the ground, don't expect me to show up and say goodbye." I hung up then tried to choke back the tears. But it was too hard. It was too painful.

Harper moved into my lap then wrapped her arms around my neck. I buried myself in her embrace and held on, clinging to the one thing I could always count on.

Harper

Whenever I was hurt, I could deal with it. There was nothing I couldn't overcome, and I never wanted someone to feel bad for me. But when the person I loved was broken and in agony, it felt a million times worse.

Troy was distraught over his brother's condition. I knew the cause of the affliction was worse than the affliction itself, and in a complicated way, Troy blamed himself. But I knew his parents' abandonment was the main cause of his grief. Like he said before, my parents weren't that warm toward me. But no matter what, they would come if something terrible happened to me. They would hold my hand and tell me they loved me, whether I was single or not.

Troy was never openly weak with me, but now he was. He didn't hide anything from me, not even his tears. The week apart had been agonizing, and when he called so late in the evening, I didn't think twice about taking the call.

And I'm so glad I did.

There were no words I could say to make him better. All I could do was sit beside him and remind him I was always there, that he didn't suffer alone. I rubbed his back and ran my fingers through his hair to keep him calm. Eventually, he leaned back and fell asleep.

Mark hadn't closed his eyes other than when he blinked. The tears would come then they would disappear again.

I stared at Troy's face and watched him sleep. I wanted to take all his pain onto myself so he wouldn't have to experience a single moment of it. But that simply wasn't possible.

But then an idea came to me.

It had a slim chance of success but I had to try. If I could accomplish it, then I would repair so much damage for Troy's family. I knew it would make Troy happy, take the burden off his shoulders as the sole guardian of his brother.

I slowly left his arms without waking him then turned to Mark. "If he wakes up, tell him I'll be right back."

He nodded his understanding.

***

It was morning when I left the hospital, and I called Aspen once I was on the sidewalk.

She answered in a raspy voice. "Why the hell are you calling me at this hour? You better be dead or something."

"I need to speak to Rhett. It's an emergency."

"He's asleep."

"Did you not hear what I said?" I hissed. "It's an emergency."

"Fine." She put the phone down then woke up Rhett. "Harper wants to talk to you."

"About what?" he mumbled.

"I don't know," Aspen said. "But it's important."

"Give me the phone." Rhett's voice came loud into the receiver. "Harper?"

"I need Troy's parents' address. Do you have it?"

"Why?"

"Just give it to me. I don't have time to explain."

Rhett seemed hesitant.

"You can trust me."

He sighed then gave it to me. "If Troy gets mad at me, this is on you."

"He won't." I hung up.

***

I arrived at their apartment and knocked. I wasn't sure what they did for a living so I hoped they hadn't left for work already. It would be terrible if they went about their day like normal when the eldest son was lying in a hospital bed.

But his mother answered the door. She wore flannel pajamas and her hair was in disarray. It was clear she just woke up. "I've never gotten solicitors this early in the morning, honey." Her tone and style of voice implied she came from wealth. There was a snooty aspect to her I didn't like at all. She kinda reminded me of my mom, actually.

"My name is Harper and I'm...Troy's girlfriend." I couldn't explain it better than that, even if it wasn't true.

His mother visibly stiffened at the revelation, and now she looked at me a different way, examining me like she was trying to commit my face to memory. "You're very beautiful, Harper."

She seemed decently nice. "Thank you..."

"I've been worried about Troy for awhile now. It didn't seem like there would be anyone else after Alexia."

I hated her name. I wasn't sure if it was from jealousy or protectiveness but I hated her all the same.

"What can I do for you?"

"Troy already told you Kyle is in the hospital. His injuries can be fixed and he will be what he once was but that's not the point. He experienced a traumatic event, and when he wakes up, he needs to see you and your husband there."

Her eyes narrowed in disapproval. Whatever support I had from her a moment ago was gone. "You're sticking your nose where it doesn't belong."

"With all due respect, ma'am, I love Troy and I will do whatever it takes to make him happy. He's really hurt by they way you've turned your back on Kyle, and honestly, I'm just as appalled. It shouldn't matter who Kyle loves or what he does in the privacy of his home. As parents, it's your responsibility to love him unconditionally. That love can't change just because he does something you don't approve of. You really should reexamine your priorities."

She crossed her arms over her chest. "You have a lot of nerve, dear." Her voice was ice-cold.

"I know. And I know you'll probably never like me now. But I couldn't care less, honestly. Please go to your son and hold his hand. Do you realize that this could have gone completely different? Kyle could have died. Or would you still not care?"

A small reaction happened in her eyes. It was slight and almost unnoticeable.

"I know you care," I said with a voice full of emotion. "I know you love him. Please let this go. If Kyle hasn't changed his mind by now, he never will. Just let him be who he wants to be."

His mother stared at me sternly, hiding her thoughts.

"Life is too short, Mrs. Sexton. You've already lost Kyle but are you ready to lose Troy too? I can promise you he'll never speak to you again if you don't go down there and make amends. And I won't blame him for that."

Mr. Sexton came up behind her. Judging the look on his face, he overheard everything.

"Please...I know you both love Kyle. Please."

She turned to her husband and had a silent conversation with her eyes.

He stared back, reading her mind.

I couldn't go back to that hospital without them. I had to make this right for Troy. I knew it really got him, right to the bone. Troy had helped me with my family. I wanted to help him in return. "Please don't make me go back there without you..."

Mrs. Sexton turned to me. "Do you think...Kyle even wants to see us?"

"Yes," I said without hesitation. "Absolutely."

She turned back to her husband. "I want to go."

He nodded. "I do too."

***

When I walked into the room, Troy was leaning forward with his hand over Kyle's. He took deep breaths like he was barely keeping himself together. I stopped and stared at him, grateful that I was about to change his life.

Troy noticed me then stood up. "Where were you?" He sounded hurt, like being apart from me was too unbearable, even though we weren't apart very long.

"I had to get something."

"What?" He came closer to me. There was a look in his eyes I'd see before. It told me he wanted to pick me up and hold me in his arms. And never let go.

His parents came into the room, and they immediately looked at Kyle, who lay like a corpse on the bed.

"Oh god..." Mrs. Sexton covered her mouth and gasped. "My boy."

Troy looked at them then did a double take. He could hardly believe they were there. "Mom? Dad?"

Tears emerged in his mother's eyes, and she didn't hide the emotion. She came to Troy then touched him affectionately on the arm. "I'm sorry we're late."

Troy's eyes shined with gratitude, and he finally seemed somewhat happy.

His mom went to the bedside and held Kyle's hand. "Honey..." She stroked his hand. "Mom is here."

"So is Dad," Mr. Sexton said.

Mark watched them and smiled.

They both glanced at him hesitantly then ignored him.

The reunion wasn't perfect but at least they were here.

Troy turned his gaze on me. "How did you...? I've been trying to get them to work it out for years..."

"I don't know," I said honestly.

He looked at me with new eyes. Like a man who'd been living in a cave his whole life, he looked at me like I was his first glimpse of the sun. His eyes took me in like he'd never really looked at me before. Adoration, affection, and something else shined deep within. He opened his mouth to speak then closed it again without saying a word. A thousand thoughts and emotions went through his mind, and there was too much to process.

Troy came close to me then wrapped his arms around me. "You are...the most amazing woman I've ever known."

I looked into his eyes and tried not to cry. It was obvious how much I loved him. It surprised me, and I almost didn't believe what lengths I would go just to make him happy. If that wasn't love, I didn't know what was. "I'm your best friend. I'd do anything for you."

"No, you're not my friend, Harper." He cupped my face then stroked my cheek. "I don't know what you are, but you're so much more than that." He leaned in and kissed me gently, not caring about his parents and Mark. They could be watching us and it wouldn't matter. All that mattered was he and I.

Gorgeous Consort

Troy

I couldn't believe my parents were there.

The last time my parents and Kyle had been in the same room together was...I couldn't even remember. But it'd been many years. When Kyle and I were growing up, I knew there was something different about him. In high school, he had a friend over and I caught them doing things in his room. I never told my parents and kept the knowledge to myself. When he finally came out and confessed his sexual orientation to the world, I felt like he was saying something everyone already knew.

Apparently, my parents were oblivious to all of it.

Ever since then, our family had been awkward. I was forced to spend the holidays with Kyle for half the time, and then my parents for the other half. And my parents pretended that was totally normal.

If they were here now, then maybe things would change.

And Harper made all of this happen. I don't know what she did or said to convince them they were being dicks, but she said something. I already cared about her and had the highest opinion of her but now...I didn't know what I felt. But I did feel something else.

I grabbed her hand and held it in mine firmly. "Thank you so much."

"I'm glad I could help."

I kissed her again, so grateful that my lips were pressed to hers. Being without her was torture, and I wasn't sure what we were now but I wouldn't let her go again. She was too precious to me.

Kyle finally started to stir and his eyes fluttered open. He took in the room around him, and when his eyes landed on our parents he blinked several times then looked away, like he thought he was making all of it up. "Mark?" His voice came out raspy.

"I'm here." Mark squeezed his hand.

"How hideous am I?" Kyle asked.

"You're beautiful, like you've always been," Mark said as he patted his hand.

"You look like shit," I said with a smile.

Kyle smiled when he heard my voice. "Go to hell, jackass."

Mom stroked his hair from his face. "You're one of the most handsome men I've ever seen—no matter how many bruises cover your face."

Kyle turned his head toward her and his eyes narrowed on her face. "Mom? You're really here."

Her eyes watered. "Yes, sweetheart."

"I thought...I was imagining it."

That made Mom cry. "I'm so sorry, Kyle. We both are." She kissed his forehead. "We're so glad you're okay."

"We are, son." Dad patted his shoulder.

"You don't hate me?" Kyle asked.

"We never hated you," Dad said firmly.

"So...you're okay with who I am?" Kyle said. "Because I'm never going to change. I hope you understand that."

"We do," Mom said. "We do."

Kyle's eyes watered and he tried to hide it. "I've wanted this for so long..."

"I'm sorry it took us forever to come around," Mom said. "But we're here now."

"And we aren't going anywhere," Dad said.

Kyle cried for a moment then wiped the tears away quickly. For being gay, he wasn't very emotionak often. He saw crying as being weak, as he told me countless times. "That means a lot to me."

Dad patted his shoulder.

"Where's my brother?" Kyle asked. "I want to see him."

I stood up then came around the bed. "I'm here, man."

Kyle's eyes lit up when he looked at me, and he extended his arm for a hug.

I leaned over and held him for a long time.

"I know you had something to do with this. Thank you."

"Actually, Harper did."

"That girl you told me about?"

"Yeah," I answered.

He pulled away and smiled at me. "She's here?"

"Hi." Harper waved awkwardly. "It's nice to meet you. I'm sorry it's not under better circumstances..."

Kyle looked at her then turned to me. That smile was still on his lips. "Troy, she's way out of your league, man."

"Shut the hell up." I laughed because I knew he was teasing me.

"She's really cute. And that's saying something since I like men."

"I know she's cute," I said. "Why do you think she's my girlfriend?" I didn't realize what I said until I already said it. It came out on its own and I couldn't rectify the words.

Kyle's grin stretched wider. "Girlfriend, huh?"

I shrugged and didn't try to fight it.

Kyle pushed me away playfully. "I want to meet my potential sister-in-law. Get over here."

She smiled then came to his side. "It's nice to meet you, Kyle. I'm sorry about what happened."

He shrugged. "You have to stand up for what you believe in. And I have no regrets. Now hug me." He extended his arm that wasn't in a cast and hugged her. "Thank you for being patient with my brother. He really is a sweet guy, underneath all that bullshit he dishes out."

I rolled my eyes and refrained from punching him.

"He's one of the sweetest and most compassionate men I've ever known. I'm very lucky to have him."

Kyle turned to me. "Don't let this one go, alright?"

"I'll try not to."

"And right off the bat, she's a million times better than that bitch, Alexia."

I didn't like hearing her name—ever. "I could have told you that."

"So there's no reason to...compare them." He gave me a meaningful look.

I didn't respond and let the comment go.

Harper came to my side and moved underneath my arm, her rightful place.

"Mom, Dad," Kyle said. "I'd like to introduce my boyfriend Mark. He and I have been together for a long time and we live together." Kyle didn't show any embarrassment or worry. He didn't seem like he cared about anyone's opinion but his own.

Mom nodded to him, awkwardly.

Dad shrugged and didn't say anything.

"Don't take it offensively," I said to Mark. "Let's just take things slow. Every beginning takes some time."

"I'm not offended," Mark said immediately. "I'm just glad you're here—whether you're glad I'm here or not."

***

My brother was discharged a few days later, and he went home with some painkillers and a cast. His arm would be back to normal in a few weeks, and I was grateful he walked away from the scene without something worse.

I was pissed off my brother was jumped to begin with, but Kyle couldn't remember any details of their faces and he didn't have any leads. It was a cold case from the beginning. But Kyle didn't seem bothered by that knowledge anyway. Knowing my parents were back in his life seemed to null out the pain from the trauma.

I finally went home and showered, and of course, Harper came with me. I got in the shower and she joined me. The warm water ran down our bodies and relaxed our aching muscles. Sleeping in a hospital chair wasn't exactly comfortable.

I stared at her perfect body and felt myself grow hard. She had a tiny waist and luscious tits. Her ass was perky and hard, and I wanted to take a bite out of it. When her wet hair stuck to her neck, she looked even sexier.

"Thank you for being there for me," I said. "I really appreciate it."

She moved her hands up my chest then massaged my shoulders. "I'll always be here for you, Troy. That's what friends do."

My hands moved to her curvy hips. "You aren't my friend."

"Then what am I?" she asked. She stared at my chest as she felt it, running up and down my sternum.

The idea of having a girlfriend terrified me. I still didn't want to do it. If Harper pulled the same shit as Alexia, I wouldn't be able to function. I'd probably become gay and swear off women indefinitely. But if I didn't give Harper what she wanted, I would lose her.

She caught the unease in my eyes. "What are you thinking?"

"A lot of things…"

"Just talk to me, Troy. You know you can tell me anything."

I tried to form my thoughts without sounding like a dick. "I know I feel something for you, a lot more than friendship. There's never been any doubt of that. When I look backward on our relationship, it's obvious, even from the very beginning, that something was between us. I can't stand the idea of you being with anyone else, and just watching Cato call you baby made me want to snap his neck. Rhett seems to think my heart beats for you, and you think the same thing. And I think...I might feel that way too."

Her hands moved down my hips where she lightly touched the area.

"But...I'm still terrified. I'm still not ready, Harper. I don't know when I'll be ready but it's not now. Perhaps I'll deny the deepest and darkest feelings in my heart because I know once I acknowledge them, I'll be lost..."

"Where does that leave us?" she asked. "Because you know how I feel about you."

I knew I felt the same way. I just couldn't admit it. "Harper, you're so much better than me. Why you waste your time with me is beyond my understanding. But I suspect you're here because...you really love me."

She nodded but didn't say the words out loud.

"I want us to be together...as we are. And one day when I'm ready, I'll give you everything you want. I just need you to be patient. It's a lot to ask, I know. But please give that to me."

"So, you're going to try?"

"Yes."

She kissed my chest. "That's enough for me."

"It is?" I asked, feeling hopeful for the first time in days.

"It's hard for me to find a man I genuinely care about. It's unheard of, actually. You're the first guy I've wanted to stick around the next morning, the first guy I've wanted to spend all my time with, and the first guy I've been able to sleep with. If there's any chance for us, I want us to try."

I cupped her face and looked down into her exquisite beauty. "I will do the best I can. Because I really want this. I really want you."

E. L. Todd

Harper

Planning weddings were already bad enough as it was. The cake had to be perfect, the right flowers had to be in season, there was the huge choice between a band and a DJ, and then, of course, the dress.

But the fact we were planning this in a goddamn month was just ludicrous.

Kara was blowing up my phone with jobs for me to do. I had to run down to the bakery while she was at work and tried to explain the floral arrangement on top for the fifth time in a row. Then I had to order the flowers for her, which cost a fortune, and then I had to sample the food without her because she was too busy getting her dress fitted. She was relying on my opinion for everything, and the pressure was going to make me crack.

And don't even get me started on the bridesmaid dresses. They were bright pastel blue, like the color of an Easter egg, and they were covered in puffy ruffles. I looked like a sheepherder wearing the damn thing. It was like she was purposely trying to make me and her other bridesmaids as hideous as possible.

Mission accomplished.

I stood in the dressing room and stared at my appearance. Even Troy wouldn't find me attractive wearing this.

"Let me see!" Kara said from outside the dressing room.

No, there are people out there.

"How long does it take to put on a dress?"

A normal dress? A minute. A blimp? Twenty minutes. I stepped out and tried to keep my dignity as much as possible.

"It's such a nice color," Kara said. "I love it."

"Yeah…" I tried not to cringe.

Kara caught the look. "You hate it, don't you?"

"No…"

"Harper?"

"Hey, it's your wedding. I'll wear whatever you want."

Kara crossed her arms over her chest. "If you really hate it, you don't have to wear it."

Was this a trap?

"What would you rather wear?"

"I'm not answering that."

Kara went to the rack and picked up a few. "I really like this one." It was deep purple and simple.

My eyes practically fell out of my head. "That looks nice…"

"Do you like it?" she asked. "Try this one instead."

That sounds too good to be true. "I'll just see how it looks…" In actuality, I was dying to put it on. I really wanted to look somewhat attractive at this wedding, especially since Troy would be coming with me. I wanted him to fall in love with me and trust me, and that wasn't going to happen if I looked absolutely hideous.

I walked into the dressing room and changed. Once the dress was on, I fell in love. It fit me just right and it made my breasts look nice without being on display too much. It was long, but not past my knees. And it was the right color for me. I had fair skin and blonde hair, so darker colors tended to look better on me. I stepped out and watched her expression.

"Oh wow, that looks amazing," Kara said.

"Please let me wear it." I was practically begging. "I want Troy to look at me and not choke on his own vomit."

She rolled her eyes. "He loves you. He doesn't care how you look one night out of the year."

"I beg to differ."

"You can wear it," she said. "It's a little more expensive—"

"That's fine," I said. I'd pay for it myself as long as I got to wear it.

***

I packed my things the night before and put the suitcases near the door. I was only bringing two suitcases since I was just there for the weekend, and I had to restrict myself on the amount of outfits I brought. As long as I had a bikini and sunscreen, I would be good for the rest of the trip.

Troy came to my door and knocked when he arrived.

"Come in," I said.

He stepped inside with one bag over his shoulder. He stopped when he saw my two orange suitcases. "You're bringing a lot of stuff..."

"And you aren't bringing anything..." I cocked an eyebrow.

"Well, I got my suit, a few changes of clothes, and my swim trunks. The rest of the time, I suspect we'll be naked." He wiggled his eyebrows at me.

I hoped we would be naked the whole time. "Well, if you forget something we aren't flying back."

"Even if I did forget something, I'll survive."

"We have a room booked at the hotel so everything is ready."

"I'll pay for it," he said. "How much?"

"You aren't paying for anything."

"Well, you aren't," he argued.

"My parents are paying for everything."

"What?" he demanded. "Your dad isn't paying for my room. And they really paid for a room for both of us?"

I shrugged. "I'm sure my parents want you to knock me up at this point. How else will I keep you around?" I rolled my eyes because my words weren't far from the truth.

"At least we'll be together for the whole trip. It's like a free vacation."

"Full of drama and gossip."

"But none of that gossip will be directed at you," he said. "Because you're taking a sexy stud along."

"Sexy stud?" I asked.

"Yep."

"That doesn't suit you at all."

"Fine, a hot guy. Whatever."

I shook my head. "You know what's really attractive on a guy?"

"What?" he asked.

"Humility."

"Humility?" he asked. "I don't even know what that is."

I believed him—without a doubt. "Of course you don't."

"Hey, you know I'm teasing." He wrapped his arms around me then moved his face into my neck. "You're the one who has something to be conceited about. You're the sexiest woman I've ever seen in my life."

"I doubt that," I said honestly.

"You shouldn't." He gave me a meaningful look. "I don't lie. Remember?"

"Have you heard of Carmen Electra?"

A shadow of a grin stretched on his face. "You think a brunette with titties that are totally un-proportional to her body is attractive?"

"You don't?" I asked seriously.

"No."

"Are you telling me you're gay? It would explain a lot."

He nudged me in the side but it was clear he was trying not to laugh. "I like real women—like you."

"You're so cheesy…"

"I'm honest," he said firmly. "If I see a girl I'm attracted to, I'll let you know. But so far, I haven't noticed anyone but you. Well, your mom is pretty hot…"

I slapped his arm. "Don't he gross."

He laughed. "You wanted the truth, baby."

"My mom is old."

"I wouldn't mind if you looked like her when we became that age…"

When he said things like this, that we would be together in the future, it made me happy but it also made me sad. Was that a realistic possibility for us? Troy said he would try, but how far would we get? He said and did everything that implied that our romance was important to him. And I knew he cared about me as much as I cared about him. Perhaps he just needed to realize it in his own way. "Let's get to bed. Our flight leaves early in the morning."

"Okay. I'll show you how much I like your average tits."

"Average?" My head snapped in his direction.

"Average size," he corrected. "Definitely not average in appearance." That stupid grin stretched his face and he escorted me to the bedroom. "Let me show you."

"You're lucky you have smooth moves."

He sucked my bottom lip as we moved. "I know."

***

The plane ride was uncomfortable and I wish we had first-class seats. I insisted on paying for the flight myself even though my dad offered. But that was why we were stuck in the rear.

I shifted in my chair repeatedly, unable to find a good position.

Troy was reading a book, and he stopped to watch me. "Having trouble there?"

"These seats are unbearable."

He moved the armrest between us then grabbed a blanket from under the chair. He folded it then placed it in his lap. "Lay down."

"Then you'll be uncomfortable the whole time."

"I'll be fine. Come here."

I was so tired that I lay down and got comfortable. My back stopped aching now that the chair wasn't torturing it.

Troy picked up his book with one hand and moved his fingers through my hair at the same time. His touch was soft like an angel wing, and he glanced down at me every once in a while to make sure I was comfortable. I'd had a few guys in my life, and Troy was the best one, hands down. He claimed he couldn't have a girlfriend, and he claimed he couldn't trust anyone, but I felt like he was already doing both things—with me.

"Are you cold or anything?" he asked.

"No. I'm perfect."

***

We arrived at the Four Seasons in Maui then retreated into our room. It was the afternoon, and half the day was already gone.

"We should enjoy the beach and surf while we can," I said. "We won't have a chance tomorrow, and I doubt we'll have a chance the day after that."

He changed into his swim trunks, which hung dangerously low on his hips, and then pulled on a t-shirt. "Excellent idea. Put on that skimpy purple bikini—or don't wear anything at all."

"It's not skimpy."

"What?" he asked. "The bikini or being in the nude?"

I walked away and didn't bother answering the question. I changed into my swimsuit and put a light dress over it. Sunscreen was lathered on my face and I was ready to go. I grabbed my bag and sunglasses. "Ready?"

"Yep."

We headed through the hotel and down to the beach.

"This place is nice," he said as he took in his surroundings.

"Yeah...Kara only gets the best." I pressed my lips together and didn't say anything else.

"You resent your sister a lot." He said it plainly, like it was the most obvious thing in the world.

"I don't resent her," I argued. "I resent my parents for favoring her and not even bothering to be discreet about it."

"I get the vibe you particularly dislike her sometimes."

We reached the beach set up, where the workers placed chairs and umbrellas in the sand. We grabbed one then sat down in the shade. "I don't dislike my sister. I guess I'm a little jealous sometimes. She's a supermodel and all the girls like her. Every time I liked a guy growing up, they preferred her the moment they laid eyes on her. It gets old."

Troy leaned back and stared at the ocean. "Your sister is beautiful, don't get me wrong, but I don't see what the fuss is all about."

"You're such a liar," I mumbled under my breath. "I don't care if you think she's hot. Just don't lie about it." *Okay, I did care but I wouldn't admit it.* Troy was the man I wanted all to myself. I didn't like the idea of him checking out other women, let alone my relative.

"You really need to stop accusing me of lying." His tone was controlled but it was clear he was extremely irritated. "Your sister is way too skinny. She's practically anorexic. I know models are photoshoped before their images are published, and let's just say that have to do a lot of work on her. Her legs have no muscle and she's just skin and bone. Some guys are into that but I'm not. Honestly, I find it unattractive. You, on the other hand, actually have muscle and curves. I'm not sure why you're jealous of her looks. You're the prettier sister, hands down."

That was the first time someone ever said that to me, and it made me feel special for the first time in my life.

"So, stop resenting her. She's very nice and it's not her fault that your parents are more proud of the fact she takes her clothes off in front of a camera than the fact you run your own business. Take it out on your parents, not her."

I knew he was right. The best thing about our relationship was the fact we would tell each other the truth, no matter how ugly it was. "I know."

"I wish you understood just how beautiful I think you are. It's not a line or a trick."

"I do know."

He turned to me and studied my face. He seemed to find sincerity. "Good." He took off his shirt. "Ready to hit the water? I read online there was a lot of sea turtles here."

"Sea turtles?" I asked in excitement.

"Let's go."

***

After being at the beach all day, we showered and fooled around before we went to dinner. There were a few restaurants at the hotel, all noteworthy for their exceptional food and wine.

We were led to a table that overlooked the water, and Troy pulled out his chair for me like he usually did

E. L. Todd

before he sat across from me. I stared at him for a long moment, unable to believe he was here with me. He was the most handsome man in the room, and he was spending the evening with me.

"What?" he asked when he noticed my look.

"Nothing," I said quietly.

He looked at his menu.

The candle on the table glowed, and the night air came through the open window. The sea was too dark to distinguish, but I thought about all the turtles and sea creatures down below.

"What are you getting, baby?" He referred to me as such more often, usually in public. I liked the name. It sounded normal, like something couples would say when they were madly in love. In my heart, I knew Troy and I could be a couple like that—if he just tried.

"Probably the sirloin."

"We're at the beach," he said. "You aren't going to get seafood?"

"I don't want to risk getting sick before tomorrow."

"Red meat is just as dangerous," he noted.

"I suppose." I looked at the menu again. "I'll probably get something vegetarian then."

Troy put the menu down. "Are you nervous for tomorrow?"

"Not really. The hotel is setting everything up and I don't need to worry about anything. I just have to keep Kara calm and breathing. That's pretty much my only job."

"Let me know if you need help with anything."

"I might need someone to vent to—that's about it."

He chuckled. "I'm here for you. And if you need a nice massage, I can help with that."

"I'll keep that in mind."

After our food was ordered and the wine was poured, we looked at each other silently.

"Thank you for coming with me," I whispered.

"My pleasure."

"You've been really helpful for the past two months. It's hard to imagine my life without you."

His eyes softened when he looked at me, and the emotion was evident.

"That week we were apart...I was lost—to say the least."

"I was lost too."

"I wanted to call you, and there were so many times I almost did..."

"Me too."

"I know this is going to sound crazy but...I really don't want to go through that again."

"I understand the feeling."

How could he agree with me but not tell me he loved me? How could he be in a beautiful and romantic place but not feel what I felt? How could he be so numb? How did one woman have the power to break him so deeply? I really hated that woman.

"Can I say something?" he asked quietly.

"Yes."

"Rhett always tells me I can have what he has with Aspen. When I look at their relationship, I see two people who genuinely care about each other. Aspen is a very nice girl and she seems very trustworthy. But I don't want what they have. I want what we have."

I held my glass of wine by the stem and stirred it.

"I just really appreciate the fact you're being so patient with me. When you brought Kyle and my parents back together...I realized just how much I was missing. You're an incredible woman. Why would I ever not want an incredible woman in my life?"

We were so close. Troy was just at the edge. He was about to trust me implicitly. All he needed was another push, another shove. "You're nothing like I thought you were. You acted like such a superficial jackass that I didn't think anything meaningful was underneath the skin. But now I see an amazing person, someone I would never hurt. You can trust me, Troy."

"I know I can, harper. I do." He gave me that sad look that told me he wasn't there yet. He wanted to be but he couldn't cross the threshold. "It's difficult to find a woman you want to spend the rest of your life with, the woman you picked to mother your children, and then have her walk away without any real explanation. I went from having life planned out to having to start over. How could I ever bounce back from that? But, my life is changing and I can see a new future—with you."

We were vaguely dancing around our true emotions. Troy gave me what he could, and I appreciated the fact he gave me anything at all.

The food arrived and we spent the evening in silence. Looks were exchanged across the table, a silent conversation ensuing. He asked me about my meal and I asked about his. The silence was comfortable, not awkward like usual, and I loved the fact he was my best friend, but so much more at the same time.

Troy

Harper was up at the crack of dawn and started to get ready. The sound of the shower and her drying her hair kept me up so I stopped trying to go back to sleep. Instead, I ordered breakfast so she wouldn't be running around on an empty stomach all day.

"Can I help?" I asked as I stood behind her and looked at her reflection in the mirror.

She was curling her hair while she wore a purple dress. "No. I'm sorry I woke you."

"Don't worry about it." I continued to stand there and just watch her.

"Anything else?" she asked.

"No." I ran my fingers through my messy hair and thought about our rendezvous from the previous night. It was more passionate than usual. Any time I looked at her, my heart rate increased slightly, almost unnoticeable. But I could hear my pulse ringing in my ears.

I was beginning to realize why I was so confused about Harper. I kept comparing my feelings for her to my relationship with Alexia. Did I like her as much? Was our relationship similar? Did they have anything in common? Alexia was the standard.

But I was quickly realizing it was the opposite way around. My feelings for Harper were a million times stronger than they ever were for Alexia. I may have loved Alexia, but whatever I felt for Harper...it wasn't comparable. I never felt like Alexia was my best friend, just the woman I loved. Harper filled both voids, and that small detail was important. Friends didn't stab each other in the back. Harper would be loyal to me no matter what. There was no reason to distrust her because what we had could survive anything.

"What?" she asked when she saw me staring at her.

"Nothing."

She continued to curl her hair but a slight smile was on her lips. "Are you going to stare at me all morning?"

"Would it bother you if I did?"

"No. But I'd like to know what you're thinking."

"My thoughts are written all over my face, Harper. Just look a little closer."

***

The wedding took place outside in the garden terrace. It overlooked the resort with the ocean in the background. It was beautiful, to say the least. Harper left the hotel room shortly after she finished getting ready and I hadn't seen her since. Now I took my place in the rows of chairs with everyone else. My mind started to drift as I thought about my relationship with Harper. Memories of our time at the beach house and my apartment came back to me. There wasn't a time when I was unhappy. That woman had the ability to always make me smile.

After everyone was seated, the wedding began. The other two bridesmaids walked down the aisle, and finally, Harper came, being escorted by a groomsmen. My head snapped in her direction and I watched her walk gracefully with the arrangement of flowers in her hand. To say she was gorgeous was the biggest understatement of the year. Her hair was down, and it trailed down her back in ringlets. Her face was highlighted with make up, and it brought out the deep color of her eyes. Her dress was tight in all the right places, and the curve of her breasts was noticeable to me and my hard cock. Harper had all the qualities of a dream girl. She was cute and pretty, but she could also be sexy as hell. Her intelligence was intimidating at times, and her wit was too quick to be competed with.

I couldn't believe I was her date to this wedding. I couldn't believe she was in love with me. And I couldn't believe she was being so patient with me. What did I do to deserve someone like her? I couldn't think of a single thing.

Kara made her entrance with her father as she headed to Sebastian down the aisle.

Instead of looking at either one of them, I looked at Harper. She watched her sister approach with love in her eyes. It was clear her sister meant the world to her, and even though she resented her at times, that love was undeniable.

Kara made it to Sebastian and the ceremony began.

I stared at Harper because nothing else could hold my interest for any length of time. I concentrated on the way her hair framed her face. The curve of her lips captured my focus, and I wanted to part her soft mouth with my tongue. Her rosy cheeks and glossy eyes were just as captivating.

She seemed to know I was staring at her because she turned her gaze my way.

My lips upturned in an involuntarily smile, and I made a discreet gesture with my hands, telling her I thought her boobs looked amazing in that dress.

Her mouth stretched into a quick grin and amusement came into her eyes. Then she dramatically rolled her eyes before she turned her attention back to her sister.

I'm in love with her.

It hit me hard and randomly, like a bolt of lightning on a summer day. It was so unexpected I wasn't sure if it was real. It just flushed through me, powerful and binding. My subconscious thoughts emerged to the surface, moving past all the doubt, fear, and distrust. Now it was the prevalent emotion, beating out all other thoughts.

I loved Harper.

Alexia wounded me and made me bleed out until there wasn't a drop of blood left. She broke my body and let my corpse rot with agony. She hurt me so much I didn't think I'd ever find myself again.

But Harper changed that. I felt like my life started over. It was a new beginning, and I was on a journey that would lead to a much different fate. There was no reason to distrust Harper because she was my best friend and would never hurt me. Is this what unconditional love felt like? Was this what happiness felt like? True happiness?

Kara and Sebastian kissed and everyone applauded and whistled. My mind was elsewhere and I had to force it to come back. I clapped even though my heart wasn't in it. I was still recovering from my epiphany, my sudden bout of reality.

***

I sat at the dinner table with Harper's parents since she was at the bridal table with her sister and bridesmaids. I didn't mind because her parents were nice people. They asked me about work and sports. They were particularly interested in my beach house, saying they were thinking of relocating in the near future.

I glanced at Harper whenever I could, and sure enough, she was always looking in my direction. I wiggled my eyebrows or winked at her. Back and forth, we flirted with discreet gestures. I couldn't wait for the dinner to end so I could be with her. Being separated from her was akin to torture.

Finally, the bride and groom had their first dance, and then everyone else was invited to the dance floor.

I left my chair so quickly it almost fell over. Then I moved for Harper, eager to reach her. I came behind her then tapped her on the shoulder.

When she looked at me, her eyes broke out in joy. It was written all over her face.

"Dance with me." I grabbed her hand and led her to the dance floor before she could answer. I spun her around then danced with her. She and I made goofy moves and laughed at each other. I could do the craziest things and she would still laugh, getting my humor like no one else did. She had some interesting moves herself, and I didn't think I could fall harder for her.

"Where did you learn to dance?" she asked as she lifted her dress then spun around.

"Dance class," I said. "It's a requirement."

"Well, you got some sweet moves."

"Watch this." I broke out in the dance moves from Foot Loose.

That made Harper laugh. "Wow, you're worth every penny."

"But I did this for free," I reminded her.

"Then I got the best deal ever."

I pulled her close and danced slowly with her, even though it wasn't a slow song. "Sorry I stared at you so much."

"It's okay. I wanted to stare at you but I couldn't as often."

"Your tits really do look amazing in that dress."

"Why, thank you. I was hoping you would notice."

"I always notice." I kissed the corner of her mouth then the other corner, wanting to give her a taste of what I wanted to do to her when this wedding was over.

"Don't tease me like that, "she said, practically moaning.

"I won't leave you hanging—later."

"You're such a jerk." She wrapped her arms around my neck so I knew she wasn't serious.

"I'm going to spank you for that comment later."

"Good," she challenged. "I like being spanked."

"I always knew I liked you, Perfect Ten."

A woman I didn't recognize approached us. I tried to pull away from Harper slightly so it wasn't too awkward. I was being a little too affectionate right now. She turned to me first and extended her hand. "I'm Kathy, Harper's aunt. It's a pleasure to meet you. It's Troy, right?"

"Yes, it is. It's a pleasure to meet you too, Kathy." I shook her hand.

She gave Harper a smile. "I think you found the one, Harper. You guys are so cute to watch."

Harper's cheeks blushed. "Thanks, Kathy..."

"Invite me to your wedding." She patted Harper's shoulder before she walked away.

Harper turned back to me, her cheeks slightly red from embarrassment. "At least I'm the talk of this party—in a good way."

"You already stole the show in that dress."

"And you did an excellent job in convincing them you're in love with me."

This was the moment. I didn't know when I was going to tell her, but now seemed like the perfect time. "It wasn't hard." I looked into her eyes and said more with just a look. "Because I am in love with you."

She stopped swaying with me for a moment, shocked by what I said and how easily I said it. The emotion moved into her eyes and she didn't try to hide it.

"I'm sorry it took so long for me to realize it. I do love you, and I've loved you for a very long time."

Her eyes watered and became glossy but the tears didn't fall.

"I'm sorry I hurt you along the way."

"It's okay," she said with a sniff.

"So, you'll be my girlfriend?" I asked.

"I already am."

"I know I can trust you." I meant those words. I wouldn't go through that pain again, not with Harper. It was different with her.

She wrapped her arms around my neck and gave me a long kiss, not caring about anyone else being there. "You aren't what I expected to find at all, Troy. You're

227

sarcastic and superficial. Most of the shit that comes out of your mouth is flat-out inappropriate. But you're...exactly what I want."

I smiled at her truthful declaration. "I know I'm a bit rough around the edges. But you soften me up, baby. But only you can pull that off."

She pulled me closer to her and rested her face against mine. The emotion passed in her eyes, and now she just seemed happy. The music played in the background and everyone had a good time, but Harper and I were in our own little world. I didn't care about anyone else there and neither did she. Time had stopped for us, and while life passed in a blink of an eye, it seemed to have no effect on us. It was our moment, and the world seemed to bow just to us.

***

I didn't rush the evening even though I was eager to get back to the room. It was Harper's sister's wedding, and I could be patient.

Even though that was nearly impossible.

We spent the evening dancing and drinking. Her family members came up to me and made small talk. They seemed to be impressed that Harper brought a date along for the wedding. I didn't understand why since Harper was a million times more beautiful than her sister. I guess beauty was in the eye of the beholder.

When the music ended at ten, the party didn't continue much longer. People started to drift back to their rooms, and the cleaning crew came out and began to clean up the massacre of garbage the party had caused.

I could tell Sebastian was eager to call it a night. He kept pulling his wife close to him and whispering secrets in her ear. Kara smiled and blushed at the same time, so I knew they would retreat to their room soon.

Finally, Sebastian convinced her it was time to end the party. "We're going to start our honeymoon." He pulled Kara with him. "Thank you for everything, everyone." He waved as he pulled her along.

Kara laughed as her husband dragged her with obvious enthusiasm.

I turned to Harper, feeling my excitement bubble to the surface. "Ready to head back to the room?" If she said no, I was going to pick her up and carry her.

"I want to hang out here for a little bit."

My eyes widened with shock.

Then a slow grin stretched across her face. "Kidding." She nudged me in the side like she always did.

I released a quick laugh then pulled her along. "I'll make you pay for that."

"But not tonight."

***

As soon as we were in the room and the door was shut behind us, the clothes were taken away. Her dress was easy to pulled off because there was no zipper. I just pulled the straps down and it fell into a heap on the floor. She wasn't wearing a bra, so I got to see her gorgeous tits right up front. I didn't want to rush this, but I was so hot for her that I struggled to slow down.

Harper seemed to have the same issue because she almost ripped my shirt as she pulled it off. When my chest was exposed, she kissed it as she fumbled with my slacks and got them undone. My hand went for her thong and I yanked it down, almost making her trip.

E. L. Todd

I steadied her before she fell, and she looked at me with amusement. "We're both a little excited, aren't we?"

"Like you wouldn't believe." I got the underwear off then kissed the area between her legs. I loved the way she tasted, like sweet watermelon. I couldn't get enough of it. It was like my hormones were synced to her exact smell and taste.

She got my slacks off then pulled down my boxers. My cock sprung free and it was clearly happy to see her. Her mouth immediately moved around it, and like a pro, she sucked.

I groaned then gripped her neck, loving the way she sucked me off. I loved foreplay with her. I could do it forever. But I also didn't like it because it might make me not last as long. While fooling around with her was fun, it didn't compare to sex.

I pulled my dick out of her mouth then moved her up the bed. I wanted the evening to be perfect. Once I was inside of her, I wanted her to never want me to leave. I wanted to feel this connection with her, to share something beautiful with her. I never realized how much of a pussy I was until then. My brother was right; I couldn't sleep with a woman unless I was in love with her. I went from fucking anything that moved to being extremely picky. I guess it wasn't a bad thing because I knew the sex with Harper would be amazing.

I realized I needed a rubber so I moved off of her to retrieve one from my bag.

She grabbed me and held me back. "I'm on the pill."

I turned back to her and moved over her. "Are you sure?" I hated wearing condoms anyway. It was like wrapping aluminum foil around your dick while fucking. It

230

decreased every sense by tenfold. Harper and I weren't a one-night stand so I was hoping she would make this offer. But I didn't expect it.

"Yes." She wrapped her legs around my waist, and the excitement in her eyes told me there wasn't a doubt in her mind she wanted this. Her hands moved up my back and to my hair as she held on.

I grabbed my shaft and pointed it at her entrance. With little resistance, I slid inside. She was slick and wet, immensely aroused and ready. The second I felt her I stopped. It felt so good I couldn't even process it. "Oh fuck..." My lips were close to hers but I didn't kiss her. I had to pause for a moment.

She seemed to be just as affected as I was. Her nails dug into me, and a quiet moan escaped her lips. One hand moved to my ass and she pushed me further inside, wanting me now.

After I acclimated to the feeling I rocked into her. Every thrust was explosive, and I couldn't believe how good sex felt. I hadn't had it in so long. But the sex with Harper was better than any I ever had. She was amazing.

"Troy..." Her voice came out sultry and sexy. It was hot as hell.

"Tightest fucking pussy I've ever had..." It was a dirty thing to say but I couldn't stop myself from saying it. Harper had to know how good she felt. She was destroying me with every thrust. My entire body was on fire and my heart was bleeding.

"You just have a big dick, Troy."

The heat was stilled for just a moment, and one corner of my mouth upturned in a smile. "It looks like we're made for each other."

She grabbed my ass and pulled me deep inside her again. "You'll stretch me out eventually."

The idea of making love to her a hundred times just turned me on more. "God, Harper. I fucking love you."

She gripped my shoulders. "I love you too."

I kissed her forehead and continued to move inside her. I grunted a lot more than I ever had during sex, but I'd never had sex with a woman like Harper. When I felt her tighten, I knew she was about to come all over my dick. I couldn't last after that. Knowing I was giving her the same pleasure she gave me was enough to break me.

Her nails dug into me, and she released a yell so loud it came out as a scream. I felt bad for our neighbors but I didn't feel bad for me. I rocked into her harder, making the bed smack hard against the headboard. I gave her everything I had, making her come long and hard. When she was finished and her nails stopped cutting into me, I tensed and released.

She grabbed my ass and pulled me far inside her, wanting me to enjoy coming into her. Her eyes burned bright with fire and she stared at me with nothing but affection.

I looked into her face as I finished, realizing it was the best orgasm I've ever had in my life. "Fuck..."

She wrapped her arms around my neck and kissed me. "Amazing, huh?"

"Oh yeah..." I breathed hard and caught my breath. But I stayed inside her.

"I'm going to sleep good tonight."

"Sleep?" I asked. "Who said anything about sleep?" I stayed inside her, and with a minute I was hard again. "We're going to be doing this all night."

Gorgeous Consort

Her eyes leapt up in flames again. "Then let's."

Harper

I was so fucking happy.

Troy and I were together, and we were starting a new relationship together. I was grateful I was patient with him even though it took forever for him to come around. Now I had what I always wanted.

Whenever I watched Sebastian look at Kara, it was with a look full of adoration. She was his entire world and it showed on every feature of his face. Now Troy looked at me that way, and I was glad I finally found the one.

For the longest time, I didn't think I would ever find the one. It was too difficult and unlikely. And when I met Troy, I definitely didn't think he was the one. Not only was he pessimistic and sarcastic, but he had more baggage than a cargo train. Dating a guy still confused over his ex wasn't my idea of a good relationship. But I did it anyway.

When I fell in love with him, it was against my will. I never expected it to happen. But I saw all the qualities that made him irresistible. He was loyal and honest, and in reality, he was extremely sweet and sensitive. He purposely tried to hide the best in him, obviously thinking it would keep people away.

That didn't work on me.

And now we both had what ee wanted.

When we returned from Hawaii, we were inseparable like always. But now we were making love all over the place. Every couch and counter was defiled. And Troy always made me come twice, making me curl my toes because it felt so good. I'd always wanted to end up with a man like that, and I was grateful that I had.

He slept at my apartment every night, and when he wasn't there, I was at his place. Like two best friends joined at the hip, we were inseparable. Now I had a dreamy boyfriend that everyone was jealous of.

There was one problem, however. He was still an escort.

"I'm not going to quit," he said firmly. "You knew this about me before we got together. I can't just walk away from this."

"I told you I was the jealous type."

"Then be jealous," he said. "But there's nothing to be jealous of. I've been doing this for years and I've never gotten involved with a client. Honestly, a girl or guy who has to pay or a date obviously has serious issues. You think I'm into that?"

I knew he wouldn't be but that wasn't the point. "I don't want you touching them."

"It's just handholding or an arm around the waist. Do you not trust me?" he demanded.

"Of course I do. But that doesn't mean I'm not jealous."

"People are jealous because they don't trust their partner. I'm the one with trust issues but I don't stress about it at all. You need to trust me too."

"Trust isn't an issue," I argued. "I just don't want girls to drool over my boyfriend all the time!"

He sighed and scratched his head. "Harper, this is my career. I'm not going to change it for you. I'm a partner in this."

"Why don't you hire someone to replace you? It'll be an extra expense but you're still pocketing the money."

"And I'm splitting my salary with someone," he argued. "Forget it. I worked hard to build this company, and I don't trust someone else to follow the rules and not get me sued. It was a promise all the guys made. I'm sorry, Harper. I love you but you're going to have to let this go."

I knew I was being unfair but that didn't stop me from acting like a brat. I sat on the couch and crossed my arms over my chest.

He sat beside me then rested his hand on my thigh. "Baby, you have nothing to worry about. I promise."

"I'm sorry I'm being weird about this..."

"Aspen doesn't have a problem with it."

"I know."

He turned my face toward him. "Please trust me. Harper, I love you and I would never hurt you. You know that, don't you?"

The look in his eyes and the words out of his mouth made me melt involuntarily. "Of course, I do."

"Then let it go. I give you my word that there's nothing to be jealous about. I like helping people and getting them through their problems. That's the part of the job I enjoy. But that's it."

"I know, Troy. I'm sorry."

"Don't apologize, baby." He kissed my forehead. "It's reasonable. I know my job is unusual. If the roles were switched I know I would struggle with accepting it. But then again, the situations would be different."

"How so?"

"A guy can take advantage of you. A girl can't take advantage of me."

That made sense.

"So...are we okay?" he asked. "Keep in mind I won't be doing this forever. I invest most of my money in real estate so when I get too old to do this I can just retire at a young age."

"That's smart," I said. "How young?"

He shrugged. "When clients no longer want to pay me."

"You'll have to sale the business to someone else or hire people to run it."

"Yeah...I'll deal with that when the day comes." He put his arm around my shoulder. "So, got plans for the weekend?" A mischievous look was in his eyes.

"I assumed I'd be spending it with you."

"How about at the beach house?"

"You know how much I love that place."

"It's a great way to land chicks." He winked at me.

"Or just one chick."

"One and only."

***

When we arrived, there were two other cars in the driveway.

"Uh...did you rent it out for the weekend and forgot?" I asked.

"Nope. We have guests."

"Who?" I asked.

"Let's go inside and see." He grabbed our bags from the trunk then walked inside.

I followed behind him then went to the back. Four people were lounging by the pool, and on closer inspection I recognized them. "Aspen?"

She sat at the edge of the pillow and let her feet soak in the water. "About time you got here."

"Troy is a slow driver," I said.

Rhett released a chuckle. "Maybe when you're in the car..."

I came closer than looked at Kyle. He didn't have any marks on his face and he looked back to normal. "Hey. How are you?"

"Great." He was sitting beside his boyfriend Mark. "My brother finally invited us over to enjoy his investment. I heard through the grapevine you've been here often."

I shrugged. "Guilty."

Aspen turned to Rhett. "You should get a beach house."

"You're the CEO of a billion dollar oil company," he countered. "You get one."

Aspen chuckled. "Touché."

Troy came out in his swimsuit. "Hey, I'd like to introduce you guys to my new girlfriend, Harper." He sat beside me then put his arm around my shoulders.

Rhett nodded in approval. "So, it's official now?"

"Yep," Troy said. "She's my lady." He rubbed his nose against mine.

"Awe," Aspen said. "I knew you guys would make it work."

"You'd be an idiot if you didn't make it work," Kyle said seriously.

Troy splashed water on him.

"Whoa, watch the hair," Kyle said. "It takes me an hour to make it look like this."

"You're such a girl," Troy said.

Kyle pulled his leg back to splash him.

"Don't you dare get my lady wet!" Troy threatened.

Kyle relaxed. "I'll get you back eventually."

Troy turned to me. "Now I'm going to be stuck to you like glue."

"Sounds good to me."

***

After spending the day at the pool we headed to the beach for a bonfire when the sun was gone. We roasted marshmallows and drank beers while we sat around. Troy made a smore and his entire face was smeared with chocolate and marshmallows. When he didn't wipe it away, I assumed he didn't notice.

"Dude, you got shit on your face," Rhett said.

Troy wiped his mouth but he missed most of the mess.

"Forget it," Rhett said with a laugh.

I grabbed a napkin and cleaned him up. "There, you're handsome again."

"I was more handsome before," Troy said with a grin.

"That's up for debate," Rhett said. Aspen was in his lap and she was curled up under a blanket.

"Want one?" Troy asked as he handed me a smore.

"No, that's a slippery slope, my friend."

"How so?" he asked. His eyes held his amusement.

"If I eat one, I'll eat five."

"That's sexy."

I rolled my eyes. "And I don't want to get it all over my face."

"Hmm..." He stared at the smore for a moment, and his eyes narrowed in bad intent.

"Don't even think about it—"

He wiped it across my face and got it everywhere.

"You son of a bitch!" I tried to smack him but he moved out of the way.

Everyone laughed.

Troy stood up then ran into the house, trying to avoid me.

I chased after him then through the house. When we made it to the kitchen I cornered him. "You're dead meat."

He smirked while he leaned against the counter with nowhere to go. "It's hard to take you seriously when you look like that."

"Aghh!" I ran to him to smack him.

But he pushed me back into the opposite counter and kissed me hard. Chocolate and marshmallow got all over him but he didn't mind. Our kiss was sweet—literally and it got heated and heavy instantly. He left me on the counter then pulled my underwear aside under my dress.

"Troy, no." I tried to push him back.

Like a mountain, he didn't move. He undid his trunks and pulled out his dick. Then he slipped inside me and stretched me.

"Someone could come inside," I said with a weak voice.

"Yeah..." He thrust into me hard and fast. "Me."

240

Gorgeous Consort

Troy

My life was awesome.

I had the girl of my dreams, the nightmares were gone, and I felt whole for the first time in years. Sex with Harper was only getting better, and now I had a woman who was also my best friend. My parents were getting along with Kyle and they were really making an effort to accept him and Mark.

I had absolutely no complaints.

Harper wasn't thrilled about what I did for a living, but what woman would be thrilled about that. I couldn't quit even if I wanted to. I had five other guys to think about, and if I dropped from the ranks, how would they fill in the hole. I loved Harper and would do anything to make her happy but I couldn't do that. Thankfully, she let it go.

I spent the next few weeks spending every spare moment with my girlfriend. I took her out to dinner, the movies, and my bed—repeatedly. Being close to another person was extremely enjoyable, and I forgot how good that felt. I never wondered if she was lying to me or if she was doing something behind my back. I trusted her, and I honestly didn't think I could trust anyone again.

But Harper changed my life.

***

When harper was at work during the day, I lay around the house and watched TV. Since I worked nights, my only time to relax was when the sun was out. I made breakfast then I watched TV until my phone rang. I knew it was Harper, asking me to go to lunch.

When I looked at the phone to answer it, I stilled.

It was Alexia.

I sat up quickly and almost fell over.

Why was she calling me?

What did she want?

Should I answer it?

Why was I panicking?

I shouldn't answer it. What could she possibly have to say to me? But I answered it anyway. "Hello?" My voice was steady and slightly angry, the usual tone I made when I spoke to her.

"Troy?" Her deep voice echoed over the phone.

"Present," I said like a smart-ass.

She paused for a moment. "How are you?"

"Why the fuck do you care?" I snarled.

"I wouldn't have asked if I didn't," she said. "And you must care about how I'm doing otherwise you wouldn't have answered the phone."

I ground my teeth because I knew she was right. "How can I help you?" Condescension was in my voice.

"I was hoping we could talk."

"I'm confused...what are we doing now?" I would never stop being an asshole to her. It was physically impossible.

"In person," she said.

"About what?" I barked. "There's nothing to say."

"I beg to differ," she said calmly. "Please just meet me. Dinner tomorrow night."

"Why do we have to have dinner?" I asked.

"Fine, coffee. Whatever you want. I really think you'll want to hear what I have to say."

I rubbed my temple because I was irritated I was still on the phone with her. "I don't think so."

"Why not?"

"We aren't friends, Alexia. We never will be."

"The conversation has nothing to do with friendship."

Her words echoed in my mind long after she said them. I hated this woman for what she did to me, loathed her, but yet, I was curious as to what she had to say. Perhaps it would give me closure. Perhaps it would help me understand why she hurt me so much to begin with. I could ask her when our relationship fell apart and what led her to find someone else. They were questions that plagued my mind for years and now I could finally reach the truth. "When and where?"

***

The impending conversation with Alexia plagued my mind all day. Stress weighed on my heart, and I felt nervous with every passing hour. What would I say and what would she say? What should I wear? How should I act?

And then there was Harper.

245

I told her everything. Should I tell her about this? I feared if I did she would get the wrong idea. She might assume I was meeting Alexia because I wasn't really over her. I was over her, and Harper was the woman in my heart. Would she understand my need for closure? Or would she push me away? I didn't know what to do.

Maybe I should tell her about the conversation after it happened? But would that piss her off even more? I didn't know what to do. I considered blowing off Alexia altogether. If it affected my relationship with Harper it wasn't worth it.

I decided it was best if I didn't tell her at all. I wasn't doing anything wrong and I loved only Harper but I had questions that needed to be answered. That was understandable, right?

But then the guilt would plague me. How would I feel if she saw her ex and she didn't tell me about it? I think that would hurt more. If I explained why I was meeting Alexia, Harper would understand. There was no romantic intention at all.

So I decided to tell her.

Harper understood me. She would know why I wanted the conversation to happen. She was my best friend. There was no reason to be jealous.

When Harper came over that night, I wasn't myself. I was dreading the conversation because I feared it wouldn't go over well. My body was tense and I felt skittish.

Harper picked up on it. "Are you okay?" She eyed me from her side of the couch.

"I'm fine," I lied. "Just a little tired."

"Well, you don't seem tired. You seem terrified."

Dammit, why did she have to know me so well? "Actually, there's something I want to talk to you about."

"Okay..." Now she seemed terrified and tense.

"It's nothing bad," I said quickly.

"Well, it's got you all worked up..."

"I'm more worried about your reaction, that's all."

"Can you just tell me?" she demanded.

"Okay..." *Here it goes.* "Alexia called me earlier today and she wanted to meet tomorrow night to talk."

Her eyes widened. "That bitch has a lot of nerve. You told her to go fuck herself, right?"

So, she was going to be pissed off. "I did...in the beginning. But she said she wanted to talk and wouldn't say what it was about."

Her eyes lit up in flames, and if she had a gun, she would shoot me. "What difference does that make?" Her hands went to her hips and she gave me a look of menace. She was tiny, but she terrified me sometimes.

"I want to talk about our relationship and where it went wrong. I want to know so I can have some closure."

She gripped her skull. "You're unbelievable."

"What?" *What did I say?*

"You shouldn't care about why your relationship ended. She cheated on you. The end."

"But I—"

"If you're over her, what does it matter?"

"It matters because I spent three years of my life with her. You don't think I haven't wondered what went wrong every single day since she dumped me? Don't you think I want to know?"

"Oh my god...you aren't over her."

"I am over her, Harper. I love you."

She covered her face for a moment like she couldn't bare it if I looked at her. "The only reason you're going is because you know she wants to get back together. What other reason could it be?"

"I don't care if she wants to get back together," I argued. "I want answers."

"Fuck you, Troy. I can't believe I trusted you."

This was going south. "Harper, calm down. I don't want her anymore. I only want you. Listen to the words coming out of my mouth."

"Your actions are more important," she hissed. "You shouldn't want to see her."

"It's not that I *want* to see her," I argued. "You're totally blowing this out of proportion."

"Am not!"

"Harper, if I was really a sleazebag that wanted to get back together with my ex I wouldn't have even told you about it. I told you why I wanted to see her. There is no other reason."

"You are in denial."

I tried to remain calm and not scream. Harper had a right to be a little uncomfortable. "Harper, I told you I loved you. Does that mean nothing to you?"

"Of course it does but—"

"You have no reason to be scared."

"This is Alexia were talking about. What if she apologizes for everything and asks for another chance?" she demanded. "This is a woman you were going to marry."

"Things change," I said simply. "I've fallen in love with someone new—someone better."

Her eyes softened for a moment and the anger disappeared.

"Harper, just because she and I are over doesn't erase what we had. Our relationship meant something to me, and I want to know what happened between us. Where did it go wrong? That relationship affects my new relationship with you. If I did something wrong, I want to know what it was. Why? Not because I still love her. It's because I don't want to make the same mistakes with you. Can you understand that?"

She crossed her arms over her chest, closing off from me. "You didn't do anything, Troy. She's just a bitch. You need to accept that and move on. You keep hoping that something is going to change, that she's going to wake up and realize what she lost. Now that you think that's a possibility, you want to see it through. If you want to get back together with her, then fine. But don't lie about it."

"Harper, I don't. Listen to me, goddammit!"

She turned red in the face. "You want to meet her so bad, fine. Go ahead."

"It doesn't mean anything, Harper. It hurts that you don't trust me."

"Well, you aren't giving me a reason to," she hissed.

Now I was getting mad. "I understand you're a little uncomfortable about the situation but you need to calm down."

"Calm down?" she asked incredulously. "You know what? Fuck you, Troy."

"Harper!"

She marched toward the door. "Have fun with the girl who fucked you over while the only woman who's ever actually loved you walks away."

I growled then grabbed her before she could storm off. "Harper, you're making this a bigger deal than it needs to be."

"Then don't go. You want me to calm down?" She got in my face. "Then don't go."

"You think I'm going to cheat on you or something? I won't touch her."

"You can cheat on someone without touching," she said. "A look is enough."

"Maybe you should take a break and cool off. Then you'll realize you're overreacting."

That didn't help the situation. "Yeah, I'll cool down," she said with a voice full of disdain. "I'll take a long break, an indefinite one, actually."

"Don't talk like that."

"Then don't see her," she countered.

"I'm just looking for closure," I argued. "Nothing more."

"Then get your closure." She walked out and slammed my door so hard I'm sure my neighbors heard.

***

I understood why she was mad. It was enough to make anyone uneasy. But she blew it way out of proportion and made it into a bigger deal. If she really thought I was going to cheat on her so easily then she never trusted me. I didn't want to be Alexia's friend and I didn't want her in my life again. Harper was freaking out over nothing

And her reaction pissed me off.

The fact she thought I would even consider betraying her hurt—bad. For a person who'd been cheated on, I definitely didn't want to do that to another person, especially to someone I loved. I didn't even want to get back together with Alexia. Perhaps Harper didn't understand my need to see Alexia because she'd never been in a serious relationship. No matter how it ended, three years was a long time to be with one person. She shaped who I was and affected my personal relationships. If I could just get some closure, perhaps I would never think of her again.

I wasn't doing anything wrong.

Was I?

***

I tried calling Harper a few times but she didn't answer. I went by her apartment but she never answered. When I went to Aspen's place, she said she wasn't there and hadn't seen her. I had no idea where she would go, but she was clearly determined to avoid me.

I couldn't sleep that night. All I could think about was Harper. This was just a fight and it would pass. I loved her and she loved me. After my conversation with Alexia, I would tell Harper nothing happened, just like I promised. Then she would realize she was making a big deal out of nothing. The anger, resentment, and annoyance kept me up all night and I barely closed my eyes for longer than ten minutes. That's how mad I was.

***

I arrived at the coffee shop late on purpose just to make a statement. I would come when I felt like it, not a minute sooner.

Alexia sat in the rear with a cup of coffee sitting in front of her. She wore a yellow sundress and the color contrasted against her tan skin. Her hair was long, longer than I'd ever seen it.

I stared at her for a moment, remembering the years we spent together. They echoed in my mind indefinitely, ringing like a distant bell. I pushed them away then approached her table. I sat down with a thud and purposely slouched. "What?" That was all I said.

"Well, hello for starters..."

"Hello," I said coldly.

She sipped her coffee and watched me with her green eyes.

"So...what's up?" I couldn't stop being hostile to her.

"I'm surprised you actually came."

"Yeah, so am I." I crossed my arms over my chest and pretended to be as indifferent as possible.

"I heard through the grapevine you have a girlfriend..."

My eyes turned to hers. Did she see us kissing in the bar that night? "Yeah, I do. I love her." I blurted it out without thinking. I wanted her to know I was happy with someone else.

She nodded but sadness came into her eyes. "I see."

"And you seemed pretty happy with your boy toy."

"That was my fiancé."

She had a fiancé? My heart sank into my stomach and I felt queasy. Someone proposed to her and she said yes? Why did she say yes to him but not to me? Why wasn't I good enough? All my insecurities came to the surface.

She examined my face. "I mean, he *was* my fiancé. He's not anymore."

Now I was just confused. "Why is that?"

"After I saw you with that blonde in the bar...and the last conversation we had...it got me thinking."

My heart slammed so hard in my chest I thought it would give out. What was she going to say? That she wanted to get back together with me? Why was my heart beating so fast? Why did I care?

"I had no idea you were going to propose, Troy. If I'd known..."

"What?" I pressed. "What difference does it make?"

"Things would have been different. I got drunk and slept with Mike because I thought you never wanted to marry me. We'd been together for three years and you hadn't even hinted at it."

"That was why?" I asked incredulously. "Because I didn't propose? Alexia, it was obvious how much I loved you. And during that time I was trying to get my business going. I didn't have the money. You know that."

"Well...I got tired of waiting."

"Why didn't you just tell me?" I demanded.

"No girl wants to talk their boyfriend into proposing..."

"I can't believe this..." I rubbed the back of my neck. "All these years I've wanted to know the answer. I never expected that to be it."

She shrugged. "Now I wish I had said something."

Silence stretched between us. I heard quiet conversations in the background along with the music. The blender would go off every few minutes. Knowing this information changed everything. If she wanted me to propose I would have done it in a heartbeat. It was weird to think how different our future would have been if I'd just known.

"I'm sorry," she whispered.

"It's okay," I said automatically. "Things happen..."

Now it became awkward.

"What happened to your fiancé?"

She shifted her weight in her seat. "After you told me you wanted to marry me and I saw you with that girl...I realized you were the only person I wanted. And I wanted to try and ask for another chance."

I froze to the spot and my heart skipped a beat. She wanted me back? She wanted to try again? She'd always wanted me but a miscommunication had ripped us apart. "Did you tell him why?"

"I just said it wouldn't work out," she said vaguely.

"But I have a girlfriend," I reminded her.

"I know...but that doesn't mean she has to *stay* your girlfriend."

I stared at her, the woman I'd wanted my whole life. Now I was sitting across from her and I could finally have her. She could be mine and we could get married. We wouldn't even have to weight.

But then something happened. "You dated this guy and told him you loved him then you dumped him for me?" Anger was in my voice. "The guy already proposed..."

"I know. I feel terrible."

"Do you really?" I said coldly.

She stared at me without blinking.

"Instead of cheating on me with some guy, you could have just talked to me. But you didn't do that. Instead, you broke my heart. How do you expect me to believe you ever really cared about me?"

"Of course I did." He eyes watered but I knew the tears were fake.

"You just want me because you can't have me," I snapped. "Now that I'm in love with someone else, you know your reign of terror is over. You want every man to be in love with you but you don't want to love them in return." I stood up, feeling stupid that I came all the way down here. Harper's words came to me. "Go fuck yourself, Alexia."

I turned and walked out, but I felt shaken. Harper didn't want me to go, and now that I sat across from Alexia I realized what happened. I wanted her to want me. Distantly and vaguely, there were feelings there. I wanted her to tell me she still needed me. It was an odd desire to have. So I was never really over her when I thought I was.

But now I was.

I had the closure I needed and I didn't want to look at Alexia ever again. She was just a mistake. I was young and stupid at the time, and my immature feelings made it seem like our loves was more profound than it really was. Thank god, I never proposed to her. I would be like her most recent boyfriend.

I stopped and turned around when I realized I forgot something. I marched back to the table and put the small box on the counter. "I can't sell it because it's engraved. And I can't throw it away. So, you can have it." Without looking at her, I walked away.

***

I searched everywhere for Harper. She wouldn't take my phone calls, she wouldn't answer the door, and no one would tell me where she was.

When I came to Aspen's door she glared at me venomously. "Please tell me where she is."

"You're lucky you're Rhett's friend. Because I would kick you in the balls if you weren't."

"I didn't do anything with Alexia," I argued. "Nothing happened."

"You shouldn't have gone at all, Troy. And we both know that." She shut the door in my face.

I went to Rhett next. "Dude, help me."

He gave me a sad look. "I don't think there's anything I can do."

"Tell Aspen to tell you where Harper is."

He shook his head. "She would never tell me because she knows I would tell you."

"Fuck." I gripped my skull and paced back and forth in front of his door.

"Troy, you shouldn't have gone."

"Why is it against the law to talk to an ex?"

"Why did you even want to talk to her?" he demanded. "What were you expecting?"

"Closure. And that's exactly what I got so I don't regret it. But I hate myself for hurting Harper."

"I don't think you can fix this."

I stopped and stared at him. "Don't say that."

"She's really hurt, man."

"I love her," I argued. "I never not loved her."

"If you guys were just fucking around like before she probably would have understood. But you've slept with her and...Harper thought Alexia was finally in the past. I don't blame her for feeling this way. She gave you everything but you lied to her."

"I didn't lie," I argued.

"You weren't really over Alexia."

I growled. "Well, I am now. I guess in the back of my mind Alexia was there but Harper took up the remaining ninety-nine percent. I'm not perfect and I never said I was.

I never even thought about leaving Harper for her. All we did was talk."

"Harper doesn't see it that way."

"Just help me!"

"I can't," he said calmly. "I don't know where she is. That's the honest truth."

"Call her for me then hand me the phone."

"I can't do that, Troy."

"Why the hell not?" I demanded.

"I'm not going to harass her for you. Remember, Aspen is my girlfriend, whose best friends with Harper. I care about her as a friend too, and I don't like what you did to her, even if you are my best friend."

"I didn't do anything wrong! You guys are acting like I fucked her or something."

"You shouldn't have gone, Troy. That's the bottom line."

I couldn't handle this anymore. I stormed off then headed to my apartment. After regrouping for a few hours, I tried to figure out where she was. I could just wait until tomorrow because she would have to head to work. But I didn't want to wait. I wanted to talk to her now.

Where would she be? She didn't have any other friends she was close to. She wasn't close to her family so I doubt she was there. Kara was still on her honeymoon. So where did she go?

Then it hit me.

She was hiding out in her office because that's the last place I would expect her to go.

***

I tried the door but it was locked. "Harper, open the door!" I banged my fists on the glass and looked inside. "Please."

She was sitting at her desk but she didn't look at me. She kept staring at her computer like I didn't exist.

"Baby, please."

Again, she ignored me.

"If you don't open this door I'm going to break it down," I threatened. "I'm not kidding. I'll pay for the damages."

She finally turned my way. "Go away, Troy," she yelled.

"No. I want to talk about this."

"Go talk to Alexia," she snapped.

"Harper, open this door now." I was sick of talking to her through glass. If she think this flimsy door would stop me from getting to her, she was stupid. "I'm going to break it down in three seconds. I'm not kidding. One...two..."

She stood up, looking irritated. "Fine."

I stepped back and waited for her to unlock the door. Once it was open, I stormed inside and shut it behind me. Now she couldn't get away. There was nowhere for her to run.

She looked at me like I was a stranger. "Say whatever you want to say and leave." Resignation was in her voice, like she didn't have any fight left in her.

"Harper, nothing happened with Alexia. We talked and then I left."

"Really?" She crossed her arms over her chest and leaned against her desk. "And what was said?"

"She explained to me why she left me."

"And did that give you *closure?*" Disdain was in her voice.

"Actually, it did. And I have no regrets."

Her eyes burned in offense. "Fuck you, Troy."

"Listen to me, I told her off then left. But I'm glad it happened. Now I understand I really meant nothing to her—now and then."

"Now you realize that?" she asked incredulously. "It didn't register when some guy fucked her?"

Her crude words didn't hurt. The idea of Alexia cheating on me didn't even make me flinch. I honestly didn't care anymore. And that was a great feeling. "I guess not."

She looked at the ground, no longer able to take in my face.

"She told me she wanted me back and she left her fiancé to pursue me."

"I bet that made you feel all warm inside," she said coldly.

"She told me the reason we broke up is because I didn't propose. She thought I never would and moved on."

"Good for you."

I ignored her jabs. "For a moment, a tiny moment, I did feel a sense of joy that she wanted me back."

Harper turned her gaze on me but there was no anger in the look.

"For just a second, I felt like she wanted me and that made me feel better. It made all the pain go away, and for the first time I could breathe again. But then I realized something worse. In a complicated way, I wasn't completely over her. But then it hit me how evil she was, what a terrible person she had become. And, like that, everything was gone. Indifference replaced all emotions. She was finally wiped away, and I walked out there without any weight on my shoulders. She's gone, Harper. Forever."

There was no joy or anger in her eyes. "So, you weren't over her just like I said."

"Partially," I explained. "Distantly. But that had no effect on my love for you. I only love you—before I spoke to Alexia and after I spoke to her."

Her voice shook when she spoke. "I was under the impression I was the only one in your thoughts when you made love to me and told me you loved me. I assumed that meant you were over Alexia completely. I assumed that night meant something."

"Don't say that," I argued. "Of course it did. Harper, I never would have done that if I wasn't hopelessly in love with you."

"But you still wanted Alexia."

"No," I snapped. "I never wanted her. I just wasn't totally over her. I think I just wanted to know why our relationship was ruined. In retrospect, our relationship wasn't even that great. It's just something I made up. Our relationship is a million times better. In the end it doesn't really matter. She's gone now and we can continue forward."

"It doesn't really matter?" she asked sadly. "No, Troy. It doesn't work like that. I worked hard to get your trust, and I put up with your baggage for this entire relationship, giving you space. But the moment you slept with me, that told me you were ready. And the fact you weren't...is just a slap in the face."

"I didn't know," I said quickly. "Honestly."

"Yes, you did, Troy."

"I really didn't. The mind is complicated and it defends itself in odd ways. But even then, Harper, you're the only woman in my thoughts. I never thought about Alexia when we were together—not once."

"Why should I believe you?"

"Because I wouldn't lie to you."

"Well, you already did," she hissed. "Now everything is out the window."

Fear gripped me when I realized she wasn't going to forgive me. "Harper, I'm sorry. I wish I could say I made a mistake and I regret it but I can't. That conversation set me free once and for all. It doesn't change how I feel about you. Please, let's start over. I'm here and I'm ready to be the best damn boyfriend in the world. I will live for you and do everything you want. Just give me another chance."

"I got hurt a lot over this relationship, Troy. But I put up with it because of the grand prize. But when I got the prize, I realized it wasn't all it was cracked up to be." She walked behind her desk and sat down.

Those words hurt—to the core.

"Just go, Troy. Please."

"Harper." There was desperation in my voice. "Don't do this..."

"It's been done," she said. "Get out of my life and stay there."

I felt the distant burn in my eyes and I willed the tears to stop. "No."

"Then I'll have to call the police," she said simply. "Get out of my office before I resort to such measures."

"Harper, listen to me—"

"You lied to me." Her hand shook on the desk.

"Not knowingly."

"Regardless, if you weren't sure, you shouldn't have fucked me like a whore."

"I didn't fuck you." My voice cracked. "If I wanted to fuck you I would have done it a long time ago. That isn't what happened. I waited until I was in love with you. That's the respect you deserved."

"Actually, I deserved a lot more than that." Her voice was barely audible.

"Don't do this," I begged. "Harper, we have everything we want now. Let's just be happy."

"No," she hissed. "*You* have everything you want. You pissed all over me on the way."

"I warned you that I had issues. It's not my fault you didn't take it seriously."

She looked like she wanted to stab me with a pen. "I've never had a problem with your issues. I would have waited forever until you were ready to be serious with me. But you rushed things when you weren't ready, and you hurt me in the process."

"I didn't rush anything. I slept with you because I loved you. If Alexia never contacted me, I wouldn't have thought about her again. You're acting like I cheated on your or snuck around behind your back. I've been upfront about everything. Would you rather me lie about seeing Alexia?"

"No, I told you I would have you rather not see her."

"And wouldn't it have been worse if I hadn't?" I asked. "Then I would have wanted to know what she wanted to discuss forever. I would have even more questions that went unanswered. By your logic, that would have been the worse of two evils. Harper, I love you but you're being unfair."

"No, you are," she said firmly. "You're *being* unfair."

"Harper, let's just put this in the past and move on."

"That's exactly what I want."

I knew she meant it in a different context than I did. "We love each other. And love can survive anything. If you think I'm just going to let you go you're sadly mistaken. I will work my ass off to get you back. I love you and I want to spend the rest of my life with you."

She looked at her desk and held her silence.

"Harper, I know how much you love me. Just give me another chance."

She sniffed as the tears emerged. "I understand that nobody is perfect, but I refuse to settle for someone who doesn't appreciate me. You dragged me through the mud and took advantage of me—"

"You took advantage of me too," I snapped. "You had me pose as a boyfriend to your family instead of just holding your head high and being yourself. You need their approval for some unfounded reason. Well, I needed Alexia's approval. It doesn't make any sense but it's just how it is. So don't act like this relationship wasn't mutual."

She wiped her tears away.

I hated to see the pain on her face. "I don't know when I fell in love with you but it happened long before I said it. I couldn't understand it at the time." My voice came out gentle. "But that doesn't make it untrue. I just couldn't process what I was feeling. I was going through a million things at once. But now that's in the past and I'm here, thinking clearly. I'm ready to love you and give you everything you want. I was always loyal to you."

"Just go," she whispered.

"No—"

"Now. I can't take this anymore…"

"Harper, we're perfect together. Don't throw us away."

"You threw us away."

She was being totally unreasonable but I didn't know how to fix it. "I don't accept this."

"That's not my problem."

My eyes burned with tears when the reality hit me. Harper was slipping from my grasp and I may not be able to hold on much longer. She was becoming more and more distant with me. The woman I loved was walking away and I couldn't figure out how to get her to stay. "I love you…" It was all I could think, a last moment of desperation.

She stared at her desk and held her silence. She wouldn't look at me, and she didn't return the phrase I was desperate to hear. A pen was in her hand and she felt it under her fingers, like she was concentrating on it so she wouldn't break down.

I knew I took the conversation as far as it would go. She was being unreasonable but perhaps it was because she was emotional. Maybe if I gave her some space she would come around. "Call me if you need me." I left her desk, feeling weak and hollow.

When I reached the door, I waited for her to tell me not to go. I waited for her to ask me to stay. I wanted to hear those words I desperately needed. But they never came. With a heart broken and severed, I left her office and tried to join society.

Harper

"You okay...?" Aspen eyed me hesitantly across the table. The right words were lost on her, and she didn't know how to comfort me. I didn't expect her to. There was nothing anyone could say.

"I'll be okay." I had to believe that so I could move forward.

"So, it's really over?" There was sadness in her voice.

"I love him but I refuse to settle."

"It's a shame," she said. "You guys were so cute together."

Every memory flooded back to me. The first time we visited the beach house together, we ended up skinny-dipping together. He took when he wasn't supposed to, but I admit, I did too. The sexual attraction was there from the beginning, but he didn't have the emotional availability I needed. But in the end, he found it. "Yeah..."

Aspen touched the side of her glass while she stared down into her beer. "Can I say something?"

"Like you wouldn't if I asked you not to," I said coldly.

"As best friends, we're supposed to say the things the other doesn't want to hear, right?"

Where was this going? I narrowed my eyes on her face and watched her carefully.

"Maybe you need to let this go..." She cringed at the end, like she thought I might break her nose off. "Troy was never whole during your relationship, and maybe he lied toward the end but I really doubt it was intentional. But now he's really over her. You can start over."

"You don't know what it's like," I said. "To stand there and ask him not to go but watch him do it anyway."

She looked down at her glass again.

"He went anyway. That's what hurts the most."

"But he didn't cheat on you and Troy isn't the cheating type."

"He still shouldn't *want* to see his ex."

"But aren't you glad he did?" she asked. "Because now he couldn't care less about her."

"I was already under the impression when we slept together," I snapped.

She released sigh, knowing I wouldn't be easy to talk down. "I've been in a few relationships and I'm going to let you in on a little secret."

"Yes, wise one?"

"Guys are totally clueless to everything around them. When they do things wrong, they don't even know it. Troy is a good guy. I know he is. He just didn't understand what he was doing and feeling. Maybe he still felt something for Alexia, however small, but it was clear he loved you. It wasn't like he lied about that."

"Dealing with his bullshit for our entire relationship was exhausting, so when he told me he loved me, I thought all of that was gone. But then to come back to New York and immediately hear him say he needs to talk to Alexia was a slap in the face." I shook my head and looked out the window.

Aspen fell silent, clearly giving up.

"Congratulations on having the perfect guy. But not everyone can have that."

"Rhett isn't perfect," she said immediately. "And that's okay. I don't expect him to be."

I turned back to her, feeling incredulous. "What's not perfect about him?"

"I'm not a fan of what he does for a living. I never ask him about it and he never brings it up because it's too difficult to discuss."

"I was never a big fan of it either."

"My point is, pick your priorities. Rhett has everything I want in another person—except that. Troy has everything you want in another person—except that."

It wasn't so simple.

"You've never loved a guy before," she reasoned. "So try to make this work."

I drank from my glass just so I had something to do.

Aspen's eyes flicked over my shoulder and saw something. Judging the look on her face, I knew what she saw.

"Troy?"

"And Rhett," she said. "They just walked in..."

"Of course they did." *That was my luck.*

Rhett and Troy came to the table, but Troy didn't look at me or speak to me. Rhett greeted Aspen, giving her a swift kiss on the lips before he pulled away. "Well, we're just here to hang out," he said awkwardly. "We'll see you around." He turned away, and Troy followed him without even glancing at me.

It hurt.

Aspen studied my face. "You wanted him to give you space."

"I know...I didn't think he would actually do it."

"Harper." Aspen gave me that firm look. "Don't be stupid right now. You two love each other so just make it work."

"I'm still mad."

"Well, be mad together. Couples don't break up every time they fight."

"Well, couples don't love someone else other than each other."

She grew frustrated. It was clear on her brow and rosy cheeks. "Harper, you're making this a bigger deal than it needs to be. I was mad at Troy because of what he did, and you deserved to be mad at him, but to dump him...that's extreme. Don't throw away a love over something petty."

"Petty?" I asked offensively.

"Yeah," she said firmly. "Petty."

I tore my eyes away from her, irritated beyond reason. Troy and Rhett were at the bar, their backs turned to us. But then I saw a brunette I recognizes as clearly as the sun in the morning. Alexia was moving toward Troy. *Why did that bitch always pop up?*

Unable to move or react, I just watched them.

Alexia stopped dangerously close to him, and Troy tensed visibly like he couldn't stand to even be in the same room with her. Then Alexia did something that made me want to chop her head off. Her eyes turned to me, and for a moment, we locked together. The look couldn't be mistaken for an accident. Then she turned back to Troy, sharing a quiet conversation.

What the hell was she saying? Was she talking about me?

"What's wrong?" Aspen asked.

"Alexia is making her move the second I vacate my spot..."

Aspen looked over her shoulder and watched the interaction. "She's not even that pretty."

No, she was very pretty. But Aspen was being a good friend pretending she wasn't. The jealous part of me wanted to walk over there and tell her to get her hands off my man, but then I remembered he wasn't my man. I had no right to do anything.

Then Troy moved away from her and walked out. He didn't look at anyone, not even me, and then disappeared from the bar. Alexia watched him leave until he was gone from her sight. Then she turned to me. The look was full of unknown thoughts, but I assumed her intent was dark.

That cunt better not even think of talking to me.

Full of grace and confidence, she sauntered across the room and headed right for our table.

"Oh shit," Aspen said. "Do not attack her, Harper. Your ass could be thrown in jail."

"For murder?" I said without any humor in my voice.

"Just walk away if you need to," she said. "That's always an option."

"You know me," I said. "I never walk away."

Alexia reached our table then she glanced at Aspen. "Hey."

Aspen just stared at her.

Then Alexia looked at me. "So, you and Troy are done, huh?"

"Yep. He's all yours, honey."

She crossed her arms over her chest, making her tits look even perkier. "I wish. But he made it pretty clear, together or apart, he doesn't want me."

I liked hearing that but I would never admit it.

"Don't tell him I said this." She suddenly shifted her weight like she was uncomfortable, and the confidence in her eyes evaporated like a drop of water on a hot frying pan. "Troy is far more in love with you than he ever was with me. I had him, and stupidly, I lost him. I wish I could get him back but I just can't. And...after everything I did to him and the way I hurt him, I want to make it right. Harper, he loves you and he's miserable without you. I'm irrelevant now. He doesn't look at me the way he used to. It's like I'm a ghost that's barely visible. You're his whole world. You really don't see that?"

I studied her suspiciously, finding it hard to believe this witch had a selfless bone in her body. "I think you're full of shit."

"Yeah?" she asked, not amused. "Well, I'm not. Did you see me try to talk to him just now? He can't stand me, Harper."

"Not many people can."

She ignored the insult. "I do have an ulterior motive for this."

"Of course, you do."

"If Troy finds out I did this for him, then maybe he won't hate me so much. So, if you do break up in the future, maybe he'll consider giving me another chance. It's my way of getting a little of his forgiveness."

"That doesn't sound selfless to me at all," Aspen said coldly.

"It's not," she said. "But everything I said is true. You're throwing away a great guy for a stupid reason. If you opened your eyes a little wider, perhaps you could see what's right in front of you." She flipped her hair over one shoulder like a trained supermodel. "Ball is in your court." Then she strutted away.

I turned my gaze on Aspen.

"I think she's telling the truth. Actually, I know she is."

"And what difference does that make?"

"Come on, Harper." She tilted her head to the side and gave me a sad look.

I finished my cosmo then looked out the window, feeling the sorrow in my heart.

Aspen sighed and dropped her look. "I hope you change your mind before it's too late."

***

A week had come and gone, and I realized just how miserable I was without Troy. The anger kept me strong in the beginning, but now I was losing my resolve. The lack of Troy was making me insane. I couldn't hold on much longer.

When I was at work, all I could think about was him. I didn't respond to emails in a timely manner, and I forgot a few appointments altogether. I was falling apart with every passing day.

My apartment was hollow and lifeless without his laugh. And when I lay in bed, I tried to pretend he was beside me, wrapped around me. It was if a piece of my heart had died and now the rest of my body wasn't getting enough blood.

Troy came to me in my dreams, and sometimes they were explicit. I missed feeling his tongue run along my body, I missed his face between my legs, and I missed the way he made love to me, giving me all the pleasure another man never could.

I missed everything.

Perhaps my emotions weren't justified. Maybe I was being unfair. I reexamined everything I once believed in. Did it really matter if he still had feelings for her? It was obvious he didn't anymore.

Unable to sit still and let another day without him pass me by, I went to his apartment. Once I was outside the door, I stood there and forgot how to knock. Minutes passed and I didn't know what to say. Should I apologize? Should I say anything? Could we just move on?

I finally found the strength to knock, and when I did, it was much louder than I meant it to be. My hands were shaking and out of my control. Self-consciously, I touched my hair and wondered if he was staring at me through the peephole. A minute passed and he didn't answer. I knocked again and feared he was mad at me. Maybe I waited too long. After I knocked a third time, I called him.

It immediately went to voicemail.

Why was his phone off? If he wasn't home, where was he? I called the one person who would know.

Rhett answered immediately. "Hey, Harper. What can I do for you?"

"I'm looking for Troy. Do you know where he is?"

"Why?" he asked calmly.

"I want to see him." My voice came out weak. "He's not home and his phone is off."

"He wanted some time alone, I think."

"Please tell me, Rhett."

He paused for a while. "You really can't figure out where he would go?"

Then it hit me. "The beach house?"

"Bingo."

***

His Maserati was in the driveway when I arrived. The house looked quiet, like nothing was happening inside. Instead of knocking, I walked around the side since I assumed he would be outside. When I reached the porch, I saw him sitting in the sand a few feet away. He was staring out at the ocean, the breeze moving through his short hair.

I stood still and watched him, seeing the sadness on his face. His lips were pressed hard together like he was tense. His body didn't carry the strength it usually did. Now he was slouching, like he was exhausted from carrying an invisible weight on his shoulders.

I eyed the pool behind him, and then an idea came to me. I tiptoed behind him then removed my clothes and set them in a pile on a chair. I stuck a toe in the water and realized it was fairly warm. Then I waded inside and put my hair in a bun. "Hey, you want to go skinny-dipping?"

Troy's head snapped backwards and he looked at me in surprise. His eyes darted to the chair where he saw the clothes sitting in a pile. Then he turned back to me. There was no amusement in his eyes, just surprise.

"Come on," I said. "Live a little." I gave him a teasing smile, trying to recreate the first time we were here.

He stared at me for a long time before he left the sand and approached the pool. He reached the edge of the concrete then look down.

I covered my goodies. "I ain't showing you nothing until you show me yours."

A light smile upturned the corner of his mouth. The happiness didn't reach his eyes, but at least he made some sort of reaction. He pealed off his clothes until he was naked then he slid into the pool. "Now let me see."

I lowered my hands and bobbed in the water.

When I looked into the water, I saw his definition. At least he was hard for me.

"Cold, sweetheart?" The cocky grin stretched his lips.

I looked down at my hard nipples. "Why don't you keep me warm?"

His eyes flashed in excitement. "I would love to." He came closer to me then pulled me against his chest. My arms moved around his waist and I felt his hard cock against my stomach. Our faces were pressed close together, and now he couldn't hide the deep sadness on his face.

Heartbeats passed, and within minutes, they synced up together. They were both dangerously slow.

"I'm sorry." He looked into my eyes as he said it. "But I'm miserable without you and I don't even know who I am anymore. I was broken when Alexia left me but...this is a million times worse. And that's because you really are the one, and you've always been the one." Sincerity shined in his eyes and he looked like he was on the verge of tears. "If you forgive me, I promise I'll be the man you want me to be. I'll give you everything, things you didn't even know you wanted. You make me so happy and I don't want to go on without you. I don't want to find someone else and try to forget about you. You'll always be the one who got away, and I'll never be able to love someone else the way they deserve. So...please give me another chance."

I wrapped my arms around his neck and felt my breasts against his chest. "I forgive you."

His chest expanded with a deep breath. "You still love me?"

"Always."

He closed his eyes for a moment, trying to gather his bearings after this announcement. He held me closer, like I might slip away. "So, we can start over?"

"I don't want to start over."

His eyes were filled with confusion.

"I want to pick up where we left off."

Finally, joy radiated in his eyes. "Yeah?"

"Yeah." I pressed a kiss to the corner of his mouth and let it linger for a long time.

He closed his eyes at the touch, like the heat of the kiss burned him.

I pulled away then rubbed my nose against his. Our bodies were combined together and our souls were connected. Our heartbeats sounded in our chest, reminding us we were alive. I didn't want to be sad anymore. I pushed Troy away when I shouldn't, and I missed him after all these weeks apart. "Have you ever had sex in a pool?"

275

The cocky smug stretched his lips. "Why do you ask, Perfect Ten?"

"Because I never have. And I'd like to try."

"Yeah?" He continued to smirk as he guided me against the wall of the pool. He pinned me back and hooked his arms under my legs, separating them. "You're in for a wet surprise." His eyes lightened at his own pun.

"Good one," I teased.

He chuckled then positioned himself before he moved inside. Then he turned serious, like he was looking at me for the first time in years. "I love you, Harper. And I want to love you forever."

My heart ached at his words. "I love you too. And I will love you forever."

Show Your Support

Like E. L. Todd on Facebook:

https://www.facebook.com/ELTodd42?ref=hl

Follow E. L. Todd on Twitter:

@E_L_Todd

Subscribe to E. L. Todd's Newsletter:

www.eltoddbooks.com

Other Books by
E. L. TODD

Alpha Series

Sadie
Elisa
Layla
Janet
Cassie

Hawaiian Crush Series

Connected By The Sea
Breaking Through The Waves
Connected By The Tide
Taking The Plunge
Riding The Surf
Laying in the Sand

Forever and Always Series

Only For You
Forever and Always
Edge of Love
Force of Love
Fight For Love
Lover's Roulette
Happily Ever After
The Wandering Caravan
Come What May
Again and Again
Lover's Road
Meant To Be

E. L. Todd

Here and Now
Until Forever
New Beginnings
Love Conquers All
Love Hurts
The Last Time
Sweet Sins
Lost in Time
Closing Time

Southern Love

Then Came Alexandra
Then Came Indecision
Then Came Absolution
Then Came Abby
Abby's Plight

Made in the USA
Coppell, TX
04 October 2023

22379226R00157